PHANTOM
HORSE

Read all the adventures of
PHANTOM HORSE

Christine Pullein-Thompson

PHANTOM HORSE

AWARD PUBLICATIONS LIMITED

ISBN 978-1-84135-820-8

Text copyright © Christine Pullein-Thompson
Illustrations copyright © Award Publications Limited
All rights reserved

Illustrated by Eric Rowe
Cover illustration by Jennifer Bell

This edition first published 2011

Published by Award Publications Limited,
The Old Riding School, The Welbeck Estate,
Worksop, Nottinghamshire, S80 3LR

www.awardpublications.co.uk

17 2

Printed in Malaysia

1

"We've got news for you," Dad said, brandishing a letter.

A new pony, I thought, and saw a spirited, grey four-year-old grazing with Moonlight and Mermaid in the paddock. My brother Angus was looking out of the window to where the lawn was dappled with sunlight.

"We're all going to Washington," Dad said.

For an awful moment I couldn't think where in the world Washington was situated. Then Angus enlightened me.

"You mean America?" he asked incredulously.

"Yes, to the United States of America, for three years," Dad replied. "We'll leave in a few months time."

I felt a lump rising in my throat. I didn't want to live in America. What was to happen to Moonlight and Mermaid? And what would we do with Sparrow Cottage?

Angus was more sensible. "What fun!" he exclaimed. "But what will we do with the ponies?

We can't take them with us, can we?"

"You can lend them to anyone you like," Mum replied. "We'll let the cottage, and you'll go to American schools."

"We'll be living outside Washington, so you'll be able to ride as long as it isn't too expensive," Dad said in reassuring tones.

"Lots of Americans ride, particularly in Virginia. I think you'll have a lovely time," Mum told us.

"We'll be going by plane!" Angus shouted. "How long will it take?" He sounded excited. I imagined him telling the boys at his school all about it.

I think I had better explain that Dad is in the Foreign Office and liable to be sent anywhere at any time. It might have been Cairo or Paris, or Pakistan or Chile or Australia. Really it was lucky for us that we were to go to America, for at least we could all go, and there would be suitable schools, and we more or less knew the language. I thought of all this as I looked at our ponies grazing in the paddock beneath tall poplars which are supposed to be dangerous, but at this moment were just turning green and looking fantastic against the shifting April sky.

We discussed America for ages and all the time I had an empty feeling in the pit of my stomach. Angus seemed terribly excited. He has Dad's mania for travel; they're really very alike, both having dark hair, brown eyes and rather sensitive faces.

I'm more like Mum, who has nut-brown hair and blue eyes. I could see that she didn't want to move either, as we all stood together in the little front room we called the playroom, on that sparkling April day.

I thought of all we would leave behind – friends, ponies, early morning rides through sombre beech-woods, hunting, gymkhanas, the Pony Club, Sparrow Cottage. I didn't think America would give us much in exchange for these. Little did I dream then of the crises and adventures which awaited us in Virginia, or that one day I should come to love the Blue Ridge Mountains almost as much as I loved Oxfordshire.

Mum told us that we were to live in a small white house in the heart of Virginia. "And you'll be lent ponies and there's a paddock and what Americans call a barn," she added, and I suddenly felt much happier.

The flight to America passed very quickly. There was a car waiting for us at the airport. We climbed inside and I must have fallen asleep immediately for the next thing I knew was Dad saying "We're in Virginia now." Then, at last, we saw our house. It stood on the side of a hill and was white, and built mostly of wood. It was called simply Mountain Farm, and I think I loved it from the first moment. Behind the house there was a building, which looked like a stable, and then a field fenced by walls. After that the land was rough and strewn with boulders until it reached the Blue Ridge Mountains, which aren't really mountains in the European sense, but more like wild, wooded hills.

We approached Mountain Farm by what Americans call a dirt road. As we drew near, I saw that a stream ran along one side of the house, and that there was a small lawn in front and some trees.

"Well, do you like it?" Dad asked.

Angus and I were very enthusiastic.

Mum said, "Don't be too pleased. We haven't seen inside yet."

"And the stables may be awful," Dad added.

There was a hammock slung between the trees on the lawn, and a garage at the back of the house.

"The ponies haven't arrived yet," Dad said, after we had put the car away. "The paddock's completely empty. I'll ring up Charlie tonight – just to let him know we're here."

Charlie Miller is an old school-friend of Dad's who married a rich American and has lived in Virginia ever since. It was he who leased us Mountain Farm and promised to lend us ponies.

The house was sweet inside, with a large kitchen, a tiny dining-room, a sitting-room and three bedrooms. There was also a bathroom, and a larder which we found already stocked with food. There was a huge piece of smoked ham hanging from a hook, a heap of American corn, a whole shelf of tins, a carton of milk, cheese, eggs and butter, and some obviously home-made bread.

It was Angus's and my first taste of American generosity and we were rather surprised.

"That's just like Charlie and Ann," Dad said.

"They must be really nice people," Angus replied. "Do you think all this stuff is really a present?"

"I expect so," Dad answered.

Mum and I started to prepare a hasty meal, while Dad and Angus carried the luggage upstairs. Mum and I cooked ham and eggs, to be followed by bread and cheese. We all felt rather sleepy, but happy, when we sat down to supper. It was nearly dark outside and the mountains looked blue, misty and romantic. Fresh air floated into the kitchen smelling a little like mountain air and, at the same time, of dry earth, boxwood and burnt grass.

When we had washed up we wandered outside to admire the landscape. It was then we heard the sound of a car coming along the dirt road and saw the flash of headlights.

"Not visitors already?" Mum exclaimed.

"It's probably Charlie. He never could wait for anything," Dad replied.

The car swung into our yard and, for a moment, we were all blinded by its lights. Then a chorus of voices cried "Hiya", and suddenly the yard was full of people. Dad was shaking someone warmly by the hand and introducing us all to Mr and Mrs Miller, who introduced their three children, Phil, Pete and Wendy. I felt in a daze and suddenly shy. The Miller children looked so old, years older than Angus and me. Wendy took charge of us. She explained that she and her brothers lived just over the hill. She asked whether the food had arrived all right and whether we liked Mountain Farm. She wanted to know whether we had enjoyed our flight and how long it had taken us to get to the house. Then Phil interrupted.

"We'll be bringing a couple of horses over for you tomorrow," he said.

Before we could say thank you, Pete said, "Has anyone told them about the wild horse?"

"No, tell them, Wendy," Phil answered.

"There's a wild horse around here in the mountains," Wendy began. I saw by the light of the headlights that she had hazel eyes and was nearly as tall as Pete, but that neither she nor Peter were as tall as Phil, who towered above us all.

"At least, he's not really wild," she continued. "He's a thoroughbred with a touch of Arab in him, and he's a palomino because of his colour. He's the most beautiful horse you've ever seen, and whoever catches him can have him, that's the deal."

Suddenly I didn't feel sleepy any more. If only Angus and I could catch him, I thought. If only . . .

"They wanted to try him on the racetrack," Pete said. "I guess he's the fastest little horse in the state of Virginia. We want you two to help us catch him. Then we can tame him together."

Charlie Miller interrupted. "Don't you listen to them, son," he said, slapping Angus on the back. "No one will ever catch that darned horse. He's as wild as they're mad and nuts into the bargain. One day someone will get up and shoot him and get a few dollars for his hide."

"Boy! You should see him jump," Wendy exclaimed, ignoring her father. "All the mares are crazy about him. They jump out of their fields and disappear, sometimes for weeks on end. That's why everyone's so mad about him."

"And remember, whoever catches him keeps him," Pete said.

"We'd love to help you," I said. "We've ridden quite a bit, though we aren't experts by any means."

"We'd sure appreciate your help," Phil replied. "With five of us we might drive him into a corral."

"Come on home," said Mr Miller. "That's enough of that darned horse for one night."

Phil, Pete and Wendy shook us by the hand before they left, and I noticed that they were all wearing jeans and checked shirts, and canvas shoes which we later learned to call sneakers.

The yard was very quiet when the Millers had gone. Mum said, "What an invasion. But it was nice of them to call."

None of us could keep our eyes open any longer. Mum leaned wearily against the garage wall. "I suppose we ought to have asked them in," she said. "We weren't very hospitable."

"I did, but they didn't want to bother us," Dad replied.

"Isn't it wonderful about the horse?" Angus asked. "Just supposing Jean and I caught him. We'd really have a horse of our own then."

I felt too tired to speak. A century seemed to have passed since we left England.

"I don't want you to do anything silly," Mum said, moving towards the house.

"Remember, this isn't England, and it's easy to get lost," Dad warned us. "Charlie's children are very anxious to ride with you and I don't want you to ride alone, for the time being anyway. Is that quite clear?"

"Quite," I replied.

"We'll remember," Angus promised.

"How about bed?" Mum suggested.

My bedroom was at the back of the house. It looked across the field to the mountains. It smelled of washed linen and boxwood. There was a painting of a horse above my bed and a pile of books on the table. The walls were white and newly painted. There were rush mats on the floor. I turned the books over and saw that they were, without exception, about horses, and that in each one Wendy's name was clearly written on the flyleaf. I realised she had left them here for me and I marvelled again at the Millers' hospitality and generosity. Had Peter and Phil left books for Angus? I wondered.

The last thing I saw before I fell asleep was a large orange moon riding high in the sky over the mountains.

2

I woke up next morning with a light heart. Birds were singing outside my window. The sky was a cloudless blue. So this is America, I thought dreamily, climbing from my comfortable bed to gaze at the Blue Mountains, serene and beautiful in the sunlight. It was still early but already there were men hurrying across the hill to the farm below – I could hear some of them singing; and from the highway came the sound of distant cars.

A girl in jeans stepped out of a van and put letters in our box by the gate. She was singing a sloppy sort of love song; she was small and active with long fair hair.

Later the Millers arrived with a clatter of hoofs which fetched us all from the kitchen where we were eating breakfast. They looked marvellous coming into the yard with the sun behind them, like something out of a Wild West film. They were mounted on a variety of horses: Phil rode a tall dun mare with a fiddle face and large ears; Wendy was on a roan pony of about thirteen hands; Pete sat astride a chestnut with a streak of white down her face.

"Hi! Are we too early for you?" Wendy cried as we emerged. "We thought you wouldn't want to wait to see your horses."

Angus was still half asleep. Five minutes ago he had been in bed fast asleep.

"It's jolly nice of you to bring them," I replied, looking at the horses Pete and Phil were leading. One was a nicely marked skewbald, the other a bay.

"I hope they're all right." Wendy sounded anxious. She looked even larger sitting astride the little roan than she had in the dusk the evening before. She was wearing a red checked shirt and the inevitable jeans; her hair appeared almost chestnut in the sunshine.

"They look absolutely super," I replied, patting the skewbald's neck.

"What does super mean?" Peter asked. Angus started to explain.

"They're nothing of the kind," Phil said after a moment. "The spotted mare's lazy and the bay mare's just a green four-year-old. But maybe you'll make something of them. They've been reared on the mountains, or near enough, and that's important because it means they know their way around. An imported horse doesn't last a month over here."

"Well, thanks very much for lending them to us," I replied.

"Yes, thanks," said Angus.

"I shouldn't say too much until you've ridden them," Phil answered, and I saw that he was laughing.

The Millers were riding on a variety of saddles. Wendy had a steeplechase saddle on her roan and rode with short stirrups. Phil was riding long with a Western saddle and wooden stirrups. Peter looked cramped on a straight-cut show saddle, which appeared out of place with the breastplate and martingale he had attached.

Wendy's eyes followed mine. She said, "We've lent you a couple of English saddles. I hope you like them."

"They're great. Much better than anything we've got at home," Angus answered.

"It's really nice of you to lend us so much," I said, looking at the horses' shoes which had calkins both hind and fore.

"We came early because in a couple of hours it will be too hot to ride," Peter told us.

"Okay, we'll dash and change. Come on, Angus," I cried, remembering that I was dressed only in shorts and a sort of sun-top.

"We won't be a sec," Angus cried, before following in my wake.

We put on jodhpurs and tee-shirts, and dragged a comb through my hair and wished that my eyes were hazel like Wendy's instead of large and blue – doll's eyes Angus called them.

When we dashed outside the Millers were calmly talking to Dad and I realised that our rushing had been quite unnecessary. They looked as though they could wait all day, quite happily chatting in the sunshine.

"The spotted mare's for you. Her name's Frances," Phil told me. He held her head while I mounted, and helped me adjust my stirrups. It felt marvellous to be on a horse again.

Frances was narrow with a prominent wither and rather long ears. Her mane changed colour halfway up her neck and three of her hoofs were light coloured. She felt tall after Moonlight and Mermaid, who are barely fourteen hands.

Angus mounted the bay. She had a well-cut, keen head and an excitable eye. She stood about fifteen one and Angus's feet only reached fifteen centimetres below the saddle flaps.

Mum appeared from the house and said, "Why haven't you put these on?" and waved our riding-hats. We had always worn them at home, but seeing the Millers dressed so casually had made us leave them where they were in our bedrooms. Now we felt foolish.

"You are twits," Mum said. "Why do you think you're less likely to have accidents here than at home?"

"It wasn't that," I replied.

"What was it then?" she asked, and we felt more foolish than ever.

"Oh, nothing," Angus said.

"Do you always wear hats then?" Wendy asked.

Hats, hats, hats I thought. Will they never stop talking about hats?

"More or less. Mum likes us to, anyway," Angus replied.

We put on our hats.

"We wear them hunting, of course," Wendy told us.

"Mind you're back by one," Dad said.

"Be careful," Mum added.

We rode out of the yard into the bright sunshine. Frances jogged. Angus grinned and said, "Our first ride in Virginia, Jean."

I felt like singing. America seemed far nicer than I had ever thought possible. I imagined the letters I would write home to my friends, Pam, Pat and June. I was certain that Angus and I were destined to be happy at Mountain Farm.

There was an odd humming noise in the air, rather like the incessant buzz of flies but with more of a croak in it and more substance. As we rode along the dirt road, Phil said, "If you're trying to guess what the peculiar noise is, Jean, I'll tell you – it's the frogs. The land around here is full of them. Sometimes you can hear them the whole night long."

I imagined thousands of frogs. "Gosh, I never knew there was so much wildlife in America. I knew there were ranches and cowboys, but I thought the rest of it was all very new and modern."

The Millers laughed.

"Not Virginia, it's tough," Pete replied, laughing at me with his grey eyes. "Why, there're wildcats and bears in the mountains."

"And deer and grey foxes," Wendy added.

"Not forgetting the wild horse we hope to show you today," Phil said.

Frances was quiet with a long, easy stride. Her long ears flopped backwards and forwards as she walked.

"Do you mind jumping a wall?" Wendy asked.

"Not a bit," I replied.

"I'd love to," Angus said.

I just had time to grab Frances's mane before we were cantering towards the one-metre wall which ran along one side of the dirt road. Frances took off rather late and I lost both stirrups and ended up by her ears. The bay mare refused, but jumped it easily when Angus tried a second time.

We cantered on across marshy land intersected by little streams. Here the frogs' singing was much louder and at intervals I saw their heads sticking out through the grass. There were

Hereford cattle grazing in the fields, and in the distance we could see tractors and men carting corn.

Frances was going beautifully, and I felt like singing as we left the flat land behind, jumped some rails in single file, and cantered up a gently sloping hill. I think Angus was finding the bay mare rather strong. He was crouched over her withers, and each time she snatched at the reins he seemed to tip a little farther forward.

When we reached the edge of the mountains, the Millers halted their horses and turned them round.

"See down there, there's your house," Phil told us, pointing.

The valley lay before us, parched and sunlit. There were cattle and stone walls, white houses, shabby wooden shacks and farms, and, farther away, the long, straight line of the highway. Our own house looked very small standing alone at the end of the dirt road.

"Nice view, huh?" inquired Wendy.

"You wait until we reach the view pole. Then you'll really be seeing something," Phil said.

Now we turned again and followed a trail. At first it was wide and grassy with trees on each side; but gradually it narrowed and there were boulders, and it twisted and turned, and low branches scraped our heads. The going became steadily worse and at one time we seemed to be riding up the bed of a stream, and twice we had to leave the path because of fallen trees. All the time we climbed up and up, and the horses sweated and the sun beat hot on our backs. We rode with long, slack reins, and our shirts stuck to our backs. Eventually Pete said, "Not much farther. My, it's hot."

We came to a clearing and there was a crash as a herd of deer disappeared in the undergrowth. There was a view on each side of us now, but the Millers wouldn't stop for us to look at it. "Wait till you get to the view pole," they said. We left the clearing and followed another rocky, winding path.

We passed a spring, and Wendy said, "This is an old Indian trail, as old as the mountains, I guess. It stretches all across Virginia right into Georgia."

I imagined Indians passing silently along the trail. "This part's got quite a history," Phil said.

We took down some rails and then we were on a wide grass track. "We've reached the gas line," Wendy told us.

"This is the way our gas comes," Peter explained.

"It must have taken years to build it," Angus said.

"It goes down almost to the river," Wendy added.

Presently we left the gas line and came to a sandy road.

"This eventually takes you to the National Parks," Phil told us.

Wendy, who was leading, turned off the path on to a narrow trail. "We've nearly made it," she said. "Be ready for the finest view in the whole doggone United States of America."

We climbed a little hill and there we drew rein. We sat limply on our sweating horses. We seemed to have reached the top of the world.

Below us, on all sides, stretched miles and miles of America. There were farms and villages, townships and towns, highways and dirt roads. There were railway lines running haphazardly across the landscape; the Potomac river gleaming faintly in the sunlight. Beyond it all were more mountains, blue and faint in the distance.

"You like it, huh?" Wendy asked.

"It's wonderful," I gasped, almost speechless. "Absolutely terrific."

"With binoculars you can see the White House and the National Monument from here on a fine day," Phil told us, with pride in his voice.

"And that's fifty miles away," Pete added.

We turned our horses and looked south, west, east and north, and on all sides the view was just as vast and breath-taking.

"It's great. I wish I had a camera," Angus said.

I was gazing at the view on the north side as he spoke, and suddenly I saw something moving, not very far away. It was moving at a great speed and, as I watched, I realised that below us was a horse galloping riderless and alone. He moved beautifully with tremendous grace. His mane was windswept and his tail streamed behind him like a pennant in the breeze. He looked like something out of another world – beautiful, powerful and alone.

"Look," I cried, pointing, "there's your wild horse." I felt terribly excited. He looked so beautiful alone in the valley.

It was ages before the others saw the wild horse. Then Phil said, "Yeah, there he goes. I wonder what happened to the two mares he had with him."

"Boy! Doesn't he look great? Wouldn't it be swell to own a nag like that?" Wendy cried.

Pete sat silent, his face set and determined. He obviously meant to catch that horse if it was the last thing he did on earth.

Angus's eyes were shining. "Isn't he wonderful, Jean?" he asked. "Just like a phantom horse."

"Has he got a name?" I asked.

"Plenty. Some folks call him one thing, some another, but they're all bad," Phil replied, turning his dun. "Come on, let's go. And I shouldn't worship that horse, Jean," he added. "He's no saint."

We rode back along the sandy road; Angus and I were full of the horse we had just seen. He was obviously a horse in a million, and I think that at that moment we were both determined that eventually he should be ours. How we would catch him when dozens of Virginians had failed was a question we didn't ask ourselves. Somehow, sometime, we would tame him and then he would be ours for ever.

"Pity he was so far away," Phil said presently. "But maybe you'll see him nearer soon. He's a great horse."

We reached the gas line and now the sun was directly overhead. Frances felt weary. She obviously wasn't very fit and the long canter at the beginning had tired her. We rode with slack reins all the way down to the valley.

"We'll take you home," Wendy said. "That is, if you won't come back with us and eat whatever's going."

"I don't think we'd better. Our parents expect us," I replied, remembering Dad's injunction about returning by one.

"It's been a lovely ride," Angus said. "Really great."

"You're very polite and English," Phil replied with a grin.

We jumped the wall again and I got left behind and jumped with the old-fashioned hunting seat. The bay mare cleared it beautifully this time, and Angus looked very pleased and patted her for ages.

"I guess we'll leave you now," Phil said.

"Well, thanks for a lovely ride," I replied.

"You're welcome. We'll be seeing you," the Millers said. They turned their horses, jumped the wall again and disappeared across the valley.

"You know, we never thanked them for lending us the horses; not properly anyway," I said.

"I shouldn't worry. I don't think Americans say thank you as much as we do. Didn't you see them grinning about me being polite?" Angus replied.

We unsaddled the horses and then we walked them into the stable. We watered them and, finding that oats had been provided as well as everything else, we gave them each a feed.

I felt very stiff; my legs didn't seem to belong to me any more. I hadn't ridden since Easter.

Mum had cooked lunch. There was sweet-corn, sweet potatoes and ham, followed by what we call over-stewed apples, and the Millers call applesauce. As Angus and I ate, we told our parents about our ride and about seeing the wild horse.

3

Angus and I spent our first afternoon in Virginia grooming the horses and helping our parents unpack. Most of the time our thoughts were with the wild horse and we were hopelessly forgetful. I put the butter in the bread-bin and a pile of books in the kitchen cupboard. Angus couldn't remember where he had put anything and dropped a bottle of tomato sauce. Altogether, we weren't very popular with Mum and Dad.

After tea, which we made ourselves, we turned the horses out in the paddock. It was much cooler. The mountains were clear of mist, and Angus and I spent some time trying to work out where we had ridden in the morning. There was no sign of the wild horse.

We ate scrambled eggs and spinach for supper, followed by peaches picked off the tree on the lawn.

I think I fell asleep that night as soon as my head touched the pillow. The last thing I can remember hearing was the frogs singing; then I was woken by the sound of hoofs and I leaped from my bed and rushed to the window. A large moon lit up the mountains. The paddock was a mixture of light and shadow. Frances and the bay mare were standing alert in the moonlight, with heads high and pricked ears. I followed their gaze and saw a horse coming across the valley. He was moving so gracefully, with incredible ease. He looked very beautiful in the moonlight. I had no doubts as to his identity.

I dashed into Angus's room. As usual he was half-buried under the bedclothes. "Wake up, wake up," I shouted into his ear. "The wild horse is here."

Angus sat up with a start; his dark hair on end, his eyes stupid with sleep. "What horse? Which horse?" he demanded. "I was dreaming of home. What are you doing roaming about in the middle of the night?"

I could have screamed with exasperation. In another moment the wild horse might have vanished and we would have done nothing but gibber in a bedroom. "It's the wild horse," I repeated. "He's here in the paddock."

"You mean he's here?" yelled Angus, coming to life at last, and leaping from his bed. "Fantastic. Quick, there's no time to waste."

"Shh. We don't want to wake up the whole house," I said, before tearing back to my own room and struggling into jeans and a tee-shirt.

I ran into Angus at the top of the stairs, hitting my hip a violent blow on the banisters.

"Do look where you're going," cried Angus.

"What about you?" I asked, nursing my hip. "It takes two to make a collision."

"Shh, there's Dad coughing. Do come on," Angus hissed, as though I had started the argument.

We tore downstairs, through the kitchen and out into the bright moonlight. We made no plans. We ran straight to the paddock. For a moment we were thunderstruck. There, standing in our own paddock, was the wild horse. He was "talking" politely to Frances and the bay mare. I noticed that his shoulder was long and sloping and his hocks low to the ground.

"I'm going to get some oats and a halter. You never know, it might work," said Angus quietly.

"He must have jumped in," I said.

I could hear the frogs, and somewhere a cow was bellowing. Otherwise, everything was miraculously still.

Angus returned with oats in a bucket, and a halter concealed behind his back. We climbed the gate into the paddock with fast-beating hearts. It seemed that our great chance had come.

Oh patient eyes, courageous hearts, I thought,

looking at the gold and flaxen horse before us.

"If only . . . " began Angus. Then the horse turned and saw us. He looked us up and down, but only for one split second; the next moment he was galloping away across the paddock followed by the two mares. I felt a wild impulse to run after him, but restrained myself.

"Why didn't you rattle the oats?" I asked Angus angrily.

"It's a bit late to say that now," Angus retorted. "Here, you have them this time."

I took the oats; but as we watched the wild horse galloping straight towards the wall, which

was all that stood between him and freedom, I knew there wasn't going to be another time. I felt sick with disappointment as I saw him prick his ears and lengthen his stride.

"He's going to jump," Angus cried, and started to run.

Another second and the palomino was in the air and jumping alongside was the bay mare. Angus gave a cry of anguish. Frances refused and then neighed frantically. The wild horse didn't look back, but cantered on towards the mountains, followed by the bay mare. For a time, Angus and I ran desperately after them, but when our legs were aching and our hearts pounding, and the horses were dots in the distance, we stopped and Angus said, "Brilliant! What are we to do now?"

"We've only got one horse left," I replied. "What will the Millers say?"

"Well, it isn't our fault. We did what we could," Angus said.

We turned dismally for home. The sound of the frogs was louder than ever, but the cow had stopped bellowing. Somewhere far away a dog barked. I saw us sharing Frances for the rest of the holidays, arguing about turns, riding and walking together across the hot, sun-baked Virginian countryside.

"Of all the bad luck! Why does it have to happen to us?" Angus exclaimed angrily.

"We'll *have* to catch him now," I said.

"But how, with only one horse between us, I can't imagine," Angus replied.

We didn't speak again until we reached the paddock. Frances was cantering up and down the wall neighing in a heart-broken way. Mum and Dad were standing in the yard with overcoats over their pyjamas.

"Oh help! Why did they have to wake up?" asked Angus.

"Just our luck," I replied.

"What *is* happening?" Dad called.

Angus and I explained what had happened. Our parents were very nice and not at all angry, though they hate us dashing about in the middle of the night.

We made tea in the kitchen and tried to decide what to do next. Dad said that we should see the sheriff and ask him to organise a really big round-up. Mum thought Frances should be used to tempt the bay mare home. We ate hunks of bread and butter, and the sun appeared with the first light of dawn in the east.

"Perhaps the Millers will have a bright idea," Dad said hopefully. "I suggest a return to bed. I'm due in Washington at ten o'clock."

Angus and I went back to bed with heavy hearts. I lay awake for ages, my head seething with pessimistic thoughts. I couldn't see how we would ever catch the wild horse. I wished that I was back in England with our own dear Moonlight and Mermaid to ride. I was much too hot in bed and being angry made me still hotter. I fell asleep at last to dream that the wild horse came into the kitchen and stole some cakes.

The sun was shining through my window when I woke up. I knew at once that I had slept late. I had a headache and felt fuddled with sleep.

I found Mum in the kitchen. Dad had already left for Washington. I made myself currant toast in the toaster and Mum boiled me an egg. Frances was standing desolately in the paddock, resting one hind leg. She obviously despaired of the bay mare's return. I started on my egg. Then the telephone rang.

Mum said, "Go on eating, I'll answer it."

I wished that I had shirts like Wendy's to wear as I looked at the scorching day outside. I felt very cross and still rather sleepy.

Mum returned. "It's the Millers for you," she said.

I suppose I shall have to explain about the bay mare, I thought, going reluctantly to the telephone.

Wendy answered when I picked up the receiver. "Hiya, Jean. Is that you?" she asked.

"Yes, hello," I replied.

"I hear you've lost the bay mare – too bad," Wendy continued. "That horse is getting a heck

34

of a nuisance – time we did something."

She said it as though we just hadn't been trying to catch him up to now. "How did you know the mare had gone?" I asked.

"One of the farm-hands saw her this morning. They were galloping across the valley together, jumping the streams like two-year-olds. Boy, it makes me mad. Anyway, you're going to have my little roan, and I'm going to ride one of the work-horses. We're coming right over," Wendy finished.

"We'll ride the work-horse. Why should you?" I said, but Wendy had already rung off.

"They're coming right over," I told Mum. "I'm going to wake Angus."

"It's going to be awfully hot for riding," Mum said.

I wakened Angus and then I rushed outside to catch Frances. She was very pleased to see me and pushed her chestnut and white nose into the halter. I led her round to the stable and gave her a feed. Angus appeared munching currant loaf.

"What's this about having another horse?" he asked. I told him about Wendy ringing up and about the work-horse. "I think the Millers are terribly generous. I expected them to be furious about the bay mare," I finished.

"Same here," Angus replied.

We groomed Frances and put on her tack.

Then we heard hoofs. "Here they are," Angus said.

The Millers were in full force. "Hello. How're you doing?" they called.

"Okay, thanks," we replied, leading Frances out of the stable.

"Here, you have my little roan, Jean," Wendy said. "You're smaller than Angus."

"I'll ride the work-horse," I replied.

Phil laughed. "You'd look mighty funny perched up there," he said.

I argued, but to no avail. Wendy had decided that she would ride the work-horse and nothing would change her decision.

"We thought we'd just hack round quietly this morning and make plans. It's too hot to go far," Phil said.

The work-mare was called Sally. She was grey and similar to a Cleveland bay in build, though a little heavier.

The Millers told us more about the wild horse as we rode across the valley.

"He was reared by an English groom. That's why we thought he might take to you," Wendy said. "It wasn't until the groom left that the trouble started."

"We speak English of a kind on account of Dad coming from the old country. But we still speak with an American accent," Pete explained.

"He wasn't so wild at first. But everyone's

chased him so much that now he's as wild as they're made," Wendy told us.

"How long has he been loose?" Angus asked.

"Since March. He's only a four-year-old," Phil replied. "The English groom had a heck of a time breaking him in by all accounts."

"Then at the end of February the groom left and after that the horse went from bad to worse. He's a mass of nerves, they say," Wendy explained.

"I don't believe he's vicious at all," Phil said.

"But don't go thinking that if you catch him, you can ride him straight home, because you darned well can't," Pete told us. "He's some horse, that palomino."

"He sounds it," Angus agreed.

"He's more a parade horse than anything else," Phil told us. "That's what they use palominos for out in California. They wear beautiful Spanish saddlery and breastplates. But he's so darned fast they thought they'd try him on the racetracks."

"I guess he would have won a race or two," Pete said.

Wendy's roan, which I discovered was called Easter, was very handy. He was half cow pony and could turn on a sixpence, though I didn't think he was very well schooled by English dressage standards.

We rode back by the village and the Millers

spent five dollars on chocolate. They pushed half of it into our pockets. They seemed to imagine that we had been half-starved since birth in England. We parted by the post office.

"I don't believe we're ever going to catch that wild horse," said Angus dismally as we rode the last piece home together. "The Millers don't seem to have any plans. We didn't really discuss it at all. We'll have to go on riding borrowed horses the whole time we're here. We'll never have a horse of our own. I know it's jolly nice of the Millers to lend us theirs and I'm being beastly and ungrateful, but riding borrowed ponies isn't like having one of your own. Is it?"

"Far from it," I agreed.

"I want to ride in gymkhanas and I don't believe the Millers ever go to shows," Angus said.

"You can't expect everything to go right from the word go. We've only been here three days," I reminded Angus.

"We'd better keep both the ponies in tonight," Angus said. "We can't afford to lose any more."

Angus and I washed up lunch and cleaned our tack during the afternoon. After tea, Dad returned from Washington and suggested that we should all spend the next day there. Angus and I were horrified. We hate towns, and large towns like Washington most of all.

"Must we? It's better here," Angus wailed.

"And it's not as though we need to buy anything," I added as I thought of trailing round crowded streets beneath a pitiless sun.

"We thought you might like to see some of the sights. There's no need to shop. I want to buy a suit, that's all," Mum said. I was beginning to feel ungrateful. I wondered why grown-ups are always so keen on seeing sights.

Then Dad spoke, "Well, I don't see why you need come if you can stay and be sensible here. The point is, will you be sensible?" he asked.

"I don't see why we shouldn't be," Angus replied, with hope in his voice. "Aren't we usually sensible?"

"I doubt it. And anyway, this isn't England," Dad replied.

"Will you promise to be sensible?" Mum asked. "That means only riding very quietly, turning the cooker off when you've finished cooking, and not speaking to strangers."

"And not going more than half a mile from the house," Dad added.

"Yes. We'll eat only bread and cheese and apples, which will cut the cooker out. We'll only walk the ponies; and we'll avoid all strangers," Angus replied.

"And we'll be generally sensible," I added.

"And not go more than half a mile from the house," Dad reminded us. "All right, you can stay."

Angus and I were delighted by our parents' decision, little knowing how, later, we would regret it. The Millers had told us that they would be spending the day visiting their grandmother in Maryland. Angus and I visualised a wonderfully peaceful time by ourselves, and we made all sorts of plans between tea and supper. "We can spend the morning schooling quietly in the paddock. I want to try Wendy's roan and I'm sure I'm not too heavy for him, if we only walk and trot," Angus said.

"And we can muck out the stable and give the ponies a really good groom," I added.

"Well, don't get kicked," Mum told us.

"Or spike yourselves with pitchforks," Dad added.

"We'll be terribly careful," Angus promised.

"If anything goes wrong, ring up Dad. We'll give you the number," Mum told us.

Angus and I retired to bed that night feeling very cheerful. Tomorrow would be our first day in Virginia without the Millers' company and, though we liked them, a day alone appealed to us as a pleasant change. The last thing Angus said to me before we parted for the night was, "One great advantage Virginia has over England is that you can depend upon it being fine."

I was to remember that remark later, but at the time I just said, "Which is really rather fantastic, isn't it?"

4

The next day dawned clear and fine as expected. The sky was a true, undiluted blue. Life seemed suddenly wonderful to us all.

We ate breakfast together in the kitchen – an English breakfast of bacon and eggs, followed by toast and marmalade. Our parents left for Washington at nine-thirty, after giving us fresh instructions about behaving sensibly. As the car disappeared along the dirt road, Angus said, "Come on, let's ride."

We had mucked out the two loose boxes earlier.

"We can groom the ponies after we've ridden. They're sure to be hot and dirty by then," Angus said, as we hurried to the stable.

We put our clean tack on the ponies. "I'll start on Easter, if you don't mind," Angus told me.

"That's all right by me," I replied cheerfully. I was feeling stupidly happy and carefree. I think Angus was too.

"I really didn't think Virginia would be so fabulous, did you?" Angus asked.

"No. I dreaded coming at times, in spite of what everyone told me at school. Of course, I still like England best," I replied, remembering Sparrow Cottage in August with the sun casting shadows across the lawn, and the sound of church bells coming across the fields, and the winding English roads.

"We really must write home about Mermaid and Moonlight soon," Angus said. "I hope they're not missing us."

"We'd better lead the ponies out into the paddock and then mount. We don't want to fall off trying to open the gate," I said.

"I wish Mum and Dad hadn't made so many rules. It's really rather tiresome. I mean just walking the horses will get really boring after a time," Angus grumbled.

"I don't think they really meant us only to walk. I think they meant that we weren't to do anything silly," I replied, opening the paddock gate.

"Well, I'm jolly well going to trot," Angus said, mounting Easter.

It was very hot in the paddock. We walked for a few minutes then we tightened our girths and trotted.

Angus, like most boys, soon tired of schooling. "Let's ride outside. It's too hot to do anything in here. Easter's dripping with sweat already," he said.

It *was* hot too – a sultry, ominous heat quite unlike anything we had yet met in Virginia.

We walked along the dirt road and then, after opening a gate, into the valley.

"We mustn't forget about the half-mile. It would be awful if something happened when we were miles from home," I told Angus.

"I'm not suggesting that we should ride far. I'm just tired of riding round and round that paddock," Angus replied.

It was cooler in the valley. A faint breeze blew from the mountains; the Hereford cattle had vanished in search of some shade. Nothing seemed to stir.

"I knew it would be cooler here. I wish we could ride in the mountains," Angus said.

"I'm jolly glad I'm not in Washington. Think of looking at statues and monuments today," I said.

"It would be the end," Angus agreed.

The ponies went well together. They were obviously old friends.

"Dad says we've got to start seeing about schools next week," Angus told me.

I didn't answer. I had just seen two horses moving across the valley. "Look over there!" I cried. "Angus, look! There they are – the palomino and the bay mare. They're heading

43

straight for the mountains." They were quite near, jogging along together beneath the scorching sun.

"Crikey, you're right. What a stroke of luck," Angus cried.

Forgotten were all our parents' instructions as we turned our ponies towards the mountains. Frances and Easter joined in the spirit of the chase. They galloped as though our lives depended on their speed.

"This may be our big chance," Angus said.

We gained steadily on the two horses until they heard our pounding hoofs, then they broke into a gallop and Frances started to blow a little. Angus said, "I hope this pony can stand my weight," and patted Easter's neck.

We jumped a wall and a "coop" almost without noticing. We reached a trail and were galloping uphill, with trees on each side of us and constant twists and turns. It was tremendously exciting. "We may not be gaining, but we aren't losing ground either," Angus cried. "Oh, if only we can catch them."

The mountains were very still, except for the sound of our pounding hoofs and an occasional sharp ring as horseshoe met rock. At first we passed cattle standing in the midst of undergrowth, their white faces besieged by flies; but gradually we left even these behind and the trail became narrower still and far more rocky. Then

the palomino left the trail, and we were galloping amid trees, banging our knees and our
heads. Frances and Easter were marvellous.
They twisted and turned, missing trees by centimetres. The ground was strewn with boulders
and they jumped some, avoided others, and
stumbled recklessly over the rest. In a few moments we were lost in a world of trees, and it
was then that I remembered the instructions that
our parents had given us before leaving for
Washington. I felt suddenly sick then and there
was a lump in my throat.

"We shouldn't be here," I yelled to Angus,
who was leading. "Don't you remember what
Mum and Dad said?"

There was a pause before Angus replied, and
I realised how completely we were lost.

"It's a bit late to think of that now. For all
we know we may be heading straight for a
dead-end. We can't afford to miss a chance,"
Angus said.

I think the devil must have possessed us then
for we galloped recklessly on, when it would
have been so easy to turn back and find our
own way home. Afterwards, Angus always said
that it was his fault, that I had wanted to turn
back. But that wasn't true. I could have spoken
then or ridden home alone. I wanted to go on
just as much as Angus did.

We left the trees at last, and started to gallop

down an old ravine; the sound of falling boulders was added to that of galloping hoofs as the horses slipped and slid, keeping their balance only by a miracle. I shut my eyes and wished that Frances had a longer neck and a better shoulder. And then it happened.

"My saddle's slipping," Angus yelled. There was panic in his voice, which echoed amid the mountains.

"Hang on to his mane," I cried, and my voice echoed too and came back to us. I had an awful sense of calamity for a few terrible seconds. Easter's head seemed to disappear between his knees. I could see Angus and the saddle disappearing with it. It was a moment I shall never forget. I saw Angus hit the rocks and the boulders, and Easter jump him and go on.

I only just stopped Frances in time. Angus lay horribly still on his side with one arm outstretched. I dismounted and Frances snorted and started to back away. She obviously had no intention of standing while I examined Angus. Fortunately there was a tree quite near; saying lots of words we're not supposed to use, I tied her to it and returned to my brother. He was breathing, though his face looked white and lifeless. I cried, "Angus, Angus, wake up," but to no avail. There was no sound but the echo of my own plaintive voice. I kneeled down and felt Angus all over in search of broken bones. I

found nothing. But I didn't dare move him, because for all I knew his back might be broken, or his neck, or his pelvis. My knowledge of first-aid was very small, but I did know that people can break bones without them showing except in X-rays, and I wasn't going to kill my brother by moving him.

But I had to do something. The sky had become overcast while we had recklessly pursued the two horses; a faint, ominous breeze stirred the trees. I didn't know where I was, nor the way home. I didn't even know the time. Easter had disappeared in pursuit of the two horses. There was only one thing to do and that was to find help. Wishing that I had a coat to put over

Angus, I untied Frances and mounted. I tightened her girth and, taking one last look at my brother, I made a detour and rode on down the ravine.

I couldn't forget what our parents had said; their words haunted me as I hurried Frances – we had promised to be sensible, we had promised to ride quietly, now we had broken nearly all our promises.

Although I hurried Frances, it was ages before we came to any clearing and then it was one I had never seen before. By this time I had decided to leave the way home to Frances. I was lost more completely than I had ever been lost before.

The sky had grown darker and in the distance there sounded the first depressing roll of thunder. Frances was marvellous. She never hesitated about which path to follow; she seemed quite tireless. I tried to memorise our journey. My mind was full of lefts and rights, of odd-shaped trees and sudden turns. And then the first sheet of lightning shot across the sky – lightning quite unlike anything I had ever seen before. It was long and jagged and, for one awful moment, it lit up the whole sky; thunder followed and then the heaviest deluge of rain I've ever experienced. Frances stopped and stood shivering. The trees seemed to tremble; the sound of falling rain blotted out everything, until the next roll of thunder came with another terrible flash of lightning.

I thought of Angus lying unprotected in the ravine. Already I was soaked to the skin. I forced Frances on into the blinding rain, down and down until the trail was suddenly familiar and I could see light ahead. I knew then that in a moment we would reach the valley. I had already decided that I would find my way to the Millers' farm. I hoped that I would find farm-hands who would come to my assistance; though how we would get Angus down from the mountain I had no idea.

We reached the valley as fresh thunder crashed and more rain fell. My shoes were over-flowing with water. My hair was plastered to my face. But I could have cheered as I caught a glimpse of what I guessed was the Millers' farm through the rain.

We galloped down a hill and scrambled over a wall, where the ground was under five centi-metres of water. The fields were deserted. The streams were running over the drive. The farm-yard was empty. Only a lone cream convertible was parked by the house. I think I started to cry then, my tears falling with the rain into Frances's chestnut and white mane.

I rode madly round the farmyard yelling "Help, help! Is anyone at home?" For a moment I didn't know what to do; then I heard the faint sound of chopping coming from a small shed at the back of the house. I threw Frances's reins over a gate and ran towards it yelling, "Help, help! There's been an accident."

I fell over a stone and scrambled to my feet again. I didn't notice that blood was pouring from one of my hands. All I could see was Angus lying white and still in the ravine.

I found a lean, middle-aged man chopping wood. I poured out my story without stopping for breath. "He may be dying by now," I finished, voicing my worst fears. "Please, please can you help?"

"You're a Britisher, I guess. I can tell that by your voice," the man said, putting down his axe. "I don't know how we'll get your brother off the mountains; it'll be real hard. If Mr Miller was at home . . . "

"Haven't you got anything which can get up there?" I asked. "A Jeep or a tractor?"

"We have a tractor," the man said slowly. "Wait a bit and I'll find George. He's the only one that can start it."

I waited in agony while he disappeared in search of George. It was still raining. A century seemed to pass before the farm-hand returned, accompanied by George, who was younger and had two fingers missing from his left hand.

"So there's been an accident," he said, looking at me. "I'll sure do my best for you, but I can't promise to get the tractor up there, not on the ground as it is."

It didn't seem to matter to them that someone might be dying up in the mountains. They didn't seem to be in much of a hurry. Perhaps they thought I was just a panicky child who got excited over nothing.

It was ages before the tractor started. The sky was quite clear by then and the sun was shining. The men hitched what they called a drag behind the tractor. It was made of wood and resembled a sledge. I collected some old coats and a couple of horse rugs from the saddle room to put over Angus. I felt calm in a horribly despairing way. Everything seemed to have taken hours. I had put Frances in a loose box, and rung up the doctor George suggested. I had found a cook in the Millers' kitchen and she had promised to have blankets and hot water-bottles waiting for Angus when he returned, also hot tea with plenty of sugar in it. She had given me brandy in a flask to try and revive him. I had meant to ring up Dad but his number was in the kitchen at Mountain Farm, and I didn't think of ringing up inquiries or the British Embassy.

George drove the tractor, I opened the necessary gates. It seemed a long time before we reached the edge of the mountains. There was a rainbow across the sky and the trail smelled wonderful. George and the other man, who was called Joe, whistled and asked me whereabouts I came from and whether I liked America. I answered "Oxfordshire" and "Yes". I was too worried for polite conversation.

I asked Joe for the time and he replied, "Two o'clock." That meant that Angus had been lying for more than two hours soaked to the skin in the ravine.

Soon we reached a place where the tractor could go no farther.

"What now?" the men asked.

I wished that we had brought a stretcher of some sort; an old gate or a hurdle would have done. "We'd better take the strongest horse rug and carry him back in that," I replied.

We left the tractor and I led the way. The men followed with the horse rug. It was very hot. The sky was quite cloudless and it was difficult to realise that there had just been a storm. Several times I took a wrong path and we had to turn back. Fortunately, the hoofprints Frances had made coming down were still visible.

At last we reached the bottom of the ravine.

"He's halfway up. Only a little way now," I cried to the men.

I wondered how we would find Angus as I struggled up the ravine, slipping and sliding on the boulders. Supposing he had regained consciousness, I thought suddenly, and started to find his own way home? The men were puffing behind. My legs felt horribly weak. I started to run. Supposing he's dead, I thought.

Angus was still lying there on his side, just as I had left him. In spite of the sun, his face looked purple with cold.

"He's quite a little guy then," George said.

"He looks real bad. How long has he been lying here?" Joe asked.

"Hours and hours," I muttered, noticing that Angus still breathed. "That's why I wanted you to hurry." I felt like crying again. I think I was nearly exhausted.

We rolled Angus carefully in the horse rug. Then we started back down the ravine.

"Do you think they'll take him straight to hospital?" I asked the men.

"I guess so. He looks real bad to me," Joe replied.

"Lying up there in the rain won't have done him a lot of good," George said.

We came to the tractor and laid Angus carefully on the drag. I covered him with coats and wondered if he should have some brandy. Then George started the engine and we began our journey down. Joe and I eased the drag over the rocks and held Angus. Even so, it was a horribly bumpy journey. We didn't talk much. I think the men were really upset now that they had seen Angus.

We came at last to the valley, and the Millers' romantic house basking in the sunshine. We could see a black car parked alongside the convertible. "That'll be Doc," George said.

Then I saw another car and I couldn't believe my eyes, because it should have been in Washington. It was our car, and nearby was an anxious crowd staring towards the mountains. I ran forward and opened the last gate, and Dad and Mum ran to meet me.

"How badly is he hurt?" they cried.

The doctor came forward and started to examine Angus. Mum explained that she and

Dad had rung Mountain Farm several times between twelve and two; getting no reply they had become anxious and telephoned the Millers. Annie, the cook, had answered and told them about the accident.

"After that we came here just as fast as we could," Mum finished.

The doctor stood up. "As far as I can judge there are no bones broken. But I'd like to get him to hospital under observation. I can take him in my automobile, I guess. I don't think we need an ambulance," he said.

"You'd better stay here, Jean," Dad said. "Annie says she'll look after you till the Millers get back. We'll fetch you just as soon as we're through with the hospital." They lifted Angus into the doctor's car, and wrapped him in rugs.

"We'll ring you as soon as there's any news," Mum said.

"Don't worry. He'll make out all right," the doctor said, patting me on the head.

Dad thanked George and Joe. Annie appeared and invited me in for a "real hot" cup of coffee and some food.

No one asked why Angus and I were riding in the mountains, instead of within half a mile of Mountain Farm.

The cars drove away. The men returned to their work. Suddenly everything was very still. I followed Annie into the kitchen.

5

The Millers' kitchen was large with windows on both sides; the floor was tiled, there was an open fireplace, a long table, and plenty of cupboards, as well as two sinks, numerous electrical gadgets and a huge dishwasher.

Annie sat me down at the kitchen table and fetched coffee, and put steak under the grill and corn on the cob on to cook.

"I'm going to give you a proper meal. You must be real hungry," she said.

I felt in a daze and very miserable. I don't think there's anything quite as bad as a really guilty conscience. I knew that soon the Millers would be home and then I should have to confess to losing Easter as well as the bay mare. Sometime I should have to tell my parents a dismal tale of stupidity and broken promises. To me at that moment the future looked horribly black, even supposing Angus wasn't seriously hurt.

Annie was very kind. She offered me more

coffee, and cake. She turned the radio on and we listened to pop music until the steak and corn were cooked. When I started to eat, I found that I was ravenous. Annie left me and started to iron in the laundry. Outside, the sun shifted to the west. I could see a lake, the Millers' long drive and the Hereford cattle coming down from the mountains. I decided that Angus must have reached the hospital, and I imagined bustling nurses and doctors in white coats. Then a car door banged and Annie hurried outside. I guessed the Millers had returned, and suddenly I couldn't eat any more.

But it was a long time before anyone came into the kitchen; not until I had washed up my coffee cup, and the plate, knife and fork I had used. I had made friends with a smiling Dalmatian by then, but I felt quite sick with apprehension.

The Millers all came in together and I knew instinctively that they had been told about the accident.

"Hello, Jean, it's nice to see you," they said. They were all rather well-dressed. Mrs Miller and Wendy were in summer dresses. Phil and Pete were in suits. Mr Miller wore a checked coat and grey trousers. It was the first time I had seen them in anything but jeans. Looking back, I suppose I must have looked a pitiful figure in comparison. My face was tear-stained and my hand had bled all over the tee-shirt I had chosen that carefree morning.

"We're so upset to hear about Angus. But don't worry, Jean, I'm sure he'll make out all right," Mrs Miller said reassuringly.

"It's wonderful what people get over. You think they're gonners and the next moment you meet them riding like the devil as though nothing had ever happened," Mr Miller told me.

"You're sharing my room," Wendy said, and she sounded pleased.

"But am I staying?" I asked. I felt very confused. Everyone seemed to be talking at once, and I wanted to confess about Easter.

"Of course you are. You're staying just as long as Angus is in hospital," Mr Miller replied.

I wasn't sure that I wanted to stay. I wanted to talk to Mum and Dad about the accident, and visit Angus in hospital, and sleep in my own bed at Mountain Farm.

"And we're all delighted to have you," said Phil, smiling.

"Come and see our room. I'm sure you'll love it," Wendy told me.

"Dad's going to ring up soon. And I've lost Easter." I confessed with a rush. "He's got all his tack on – that's the awful part."

I felt like crying. The Millers didn't seem to realise how dreadful the day had been. They were cheerful and kind; but I wanted someone who would say that everything hadn't been my fault, that no one could have done more than I had, that they were certain Angus would soon recover and that Easter would come home.

"Don't you worry about that. Easter can look after himself," Mr Miller replied, patting me on the back.

"We'll start thinking about him tomorrow," Mrs Miller said.

"But shouldn't we look for him? He might get hung up or something," I said.

The Millers laughed. "Not him. It's not the first time he's spent a night on the mountains," Wendy answered.

Then the telephone rang. "That's for me," I cried, running into a spacious hall hung with sporting prints.

"It's in the room on the right," Phil called.

I found the telephone, but it wasn't Dad. A voice said, "Is Mr Miller there?"

"Yes, I'll fetch him," I replied, and fled back to the kitchen.

I was terribly disappointed. Wendy took me to her room which, like the kitchen, had windows on both sides.

There were two beds, lots of furniture, a television set and a radio. The beds had bright bedspreads and the curtains were made of checked cotton cloth.

"How do you like it?" Wendy asked.

"It's lovely," I replied, and then I sat down on the nearest bed and started to cry.

Wendy didn't know what to do. She shut all the windows and turned over some papers on a desk. She put away a pair of jeans which were lying on the floor. Then she said, "Don't worry, Jean. I know your brother's going to be all right. Of course he is," but she didn't sound at all certain.

"The awful part is we weren't supposed to ride farther than half a mile from the house," I confessed. Then I told her the whole story.

When I had finished Wendy said, "We all do silly things sometimes in our lives. You were just unlucky. Boy, when I think of some of the things I've done . . . Far worse things than riding farther than I was told. Honestly, Jean, I've got away with murder. Don't you know the saying, 'Who never makes mistakes never makes anything.' Dad is always quoting it."

As Wendy spoke, I decided that she was a great deal nicer than I had suspected. Then the telephone started to ring again.

"That *must* be Dad," I cried, leaping to my feet. I felt horribly weak as I ran downstairs. I didn't dare imagine what Dad might have to say.

Mr Miller was speaking. "Yes, she's still here. We thought she might stay the night. Sure. No trouble at all. Hang on . . . Here, it's for you," he said, passing the receiver over to me.

"Hello, is that Jean?" Dad asked.

I could hear my heart beating. "Yes," I answered, and my voice came out very small. "How's Angus?"

"Much better. He's conscious. He's to stay here for another twenty-four hours at least, but they can't find any broken bones or anything. At the moment he can't remember what exactly happened, but he's quite cheerful now and asking about you."

I felt immensely relieved; nothing mattered much now that I knew Angus was recovering.

"Are you all right?" Dad continued. "Charlie has kindly said that you can stay with them."

"I'm quite all right, thank you. And very relieved about Angus," I replied.

"Here's Mum," Dad said.

"Hello, isn't it wonderful about Angus?" Mum asked. "We're terribly pleased. Are you all right?"

"Yes, quite okay," I said.

"We're going to stay here overnight," Mum told me. "We hope to bring Angus back quite soon but the doctor doesn't want him moved until he's got over the concussion. At present he's lying in a darkened room."

"I'm terribly sorry it happened," I apologised.

"We can't see how it did," Mum replied cheerfully. "Never mind, you can explain it all

later. The great thing is Angus is okay." Mum chatted for a few minutes, then rang off.

"Is he all right?" Mrs Miller asked.

I told the Millers everything my parents had said. Then Phil introduced me to the dogs: Cop, the Dalmatian I had already met; Maggie, a little cairn; and Susie, a sweet fox-terrier with a large patch of black over one eye. They all seemed to belong to everyone. Pete had disappeared. Outside a breeze stirred the apple-trees, which were scattered at intervals across the lawn. The sun was setting. A Jeep full of farm-hands was disappearing along the drive.

"Tomorrow we'll have a round-up. We can't miss the opportunity, having Jean here," Mr Miller said.

"But what about the horses? We haven't got enough to go round now," Wendy replied. "Frances must rest tomorrow, she's dog-tired."

I thought of the bay mare and Easter roaming the mountains together.

"What's wrong with old Pelican?" Mr Miller asked.

"But he hasn't been ridden for such a heck of a long time," Wendy replied.

"It'll do him good to have some work," Mr Miller answered.

"Jean can have my mare. I don't mind riding Pelican," Phil said.

"I shall ride Sally," Wendy told us.

I couldn't see myself riding Phil's dun mare. But I didn't say anything. I felt I must ride who I was told, particularly since Angus and I were responsible for the loss of two horses already.

The Millers were really kind. At dinner they gave me the best piece of the rib roast and afterwards, when everybody drank coffee, I was provided with a cup of tea. Pete gave me a large box of chocolates, which he had bought in the village while I was being introduced to the dogs. Phil presented me with one of his fountain-pens and Wendy showed me all her horsy books which weren't in my bedroom at Mountain Farm.

After we had eaten, we all watched television in Wendy's room. I thought I wouldn't sleep;

but when eventually I went to bed, sometime between eleven and twelve, I fell asleep immediately and didn't dream at all.

Morning came bright and early in Wendy's room. A light breeze stirred the checked curtains, lazy clouds drifted across a blue sky; I could hear the men fetching the cows and the singing of the frogs in the lowland.

Wendy was still sleeping, one arm tangled in her red-brown hair. Birds were arguing in the apple-trees on the lawn; the lake and streams shone silver and gold in the sunlight. I could hear Annie putting the kettle on to boil in the kitchen. Someone was running taps in the bathroom. I couldn't bear to stay in bed a moment longer. I dressed quickly and hurried downstairs.

I wandered outside. Secretly, I hoped that Easter would have returned, but there was no sign of him. Pete was catching the horses.

"Hello, Jean," he called. "You're up early. The others are still in bed." Pete was unusually cheerful. "I'm crazy about the early morning. It's the finest part of the day. When I've finished with school and college I'm going to farm," he told me.

Pete whistled for the horses and they trotted across the paddock. He had the three dogs at his heels. We led the horses in with just our arms round their necks. When they were all in the stables, we gave them each a feed of oats.

Pete said, "I bet Phil's mad. He hates round-ups. I'm the only one who cares about them."

I was seeing Pete in a new light. He seemed a different person by himself. He hadn't Phil's glamorous good looks – Phil one could imagine being a film star, a dashing officer in uniform, a pilot, a racing driver – but he cared more about things. I knew that Pete would rather die than part with an old favourite. He would hang on to a farm he loved obstinately in the face of extreme poverty. Money would mean little to Pete, beyond new fences for his farm, I decided.

We watched the horses eating. "I'm going to send my chestnut mare to stud. I think she should breed a nice foal," Pete said.

Pelican was a lean, grey horse with a wall-eye. He was heavily scarred, and he watched us warily out of his good eye as he munched his feed.

"He's never been much good. He's too darned cunning," Pete told me.

We ate breakfast in the long dining-room where we had eaten supper the night before. There were waffles and bacon, loads of home-made bread and dairy butter. Phil hardly ate anything. Pete devoured nine waffles; Wendy ate mostly bread. I tried the waffles, eating them in the traditional manner with butter, syrup and bacon. Personally, I like them better without the bacon, which I didn't think mixed well with the syrup. As we ate we discussed the round-up. We were to start by riding to given spots in the mountains. There was some argument as to which horses we were to ride. I remained silent. I was now suddenly determined to ride Pelican. Once we had reached our given spots, we were to ride down, driving any cattle we met before us.

"They're never much trouble till you reach the lower meadows, Jean. Then they're a heck of a lot," Mr Miller told me.

"We drive them all in and separate them afterwards in the loading pens," Pete explained.

"The men will all be waiting for you at the field gate," Mr Miller said.

We carried the breakfast things through to the kitchen and put them in the dishwasher before hurrying to the stable yard. The horses had finished eating. I decided to take the bull by the horns. "I'm riding Pelican," I stated firmly. "It's my fault you are two horses short. It's quite obvious that I'm the person who should ride him, and anyway, I'd just as soon ride him as the dun mare." I said it with rather a rush and Phil began to laugh.

"You sound as though you've made up your mind all right," he said. "But you know he's a bit of a rogue, Jean, don't you?" Pete asked, and he sounded worried.

"I don't care. I'm going to ride him," I

replied. Phil shrugged his shoulders. "When women make up their minds . . . " he said.

"We don't want another accident," Pete said.

"Suits me all right. I'd much rather ride my dun," Phil told us, whistling cheerfully.

"What does Pelican do, anyway?" I asked Pete. "He doesn't look vicious."

"One never knows. I think he's nuts," Pete replied.

We collected our tack from the saddle room. I was given the choice of a gag and curb, or a pelham, but I turned them both down and chose a snaffle. I think the Millers were rather surprised. I explained that my hands weren't particularly good, and that I had often been told that difficult horses were happiest in snaffles. I refused the offer of a martingale. If Pelican's neck had been strong and heavy I don't know which bridle I would have chosen. But he didn't look like a puller. He looked more like a horse which would go behind his bit and rear.

We didn't bother to groom the horses. Pete helped me bridle Pelican. Then we led the horses out and mounted. Pelican felt tall and bony. I could feel him watching me with his good eye, and his ears were back.

"Be careful, Jean. He reared here once," Pete said.

"I'm glad I chose this old plug. I love her,"

Wendy told us, leaning forward and patting Sally.

Pelican followed the other horses with short, uneasy steps. I gave him his head and hoped that nothing would go wrong. I didn't wish to be in hospital as well as Angus, and Pete's obvious anxiety made me wonder what Pelican had done in the past to earn himself such a bad name.

It was a wonderful day. There were still clouds in the sky, and a light breeze fanned our faces as we rode across the valley. Pelican started to relax and the Millers ceased watching me anxiously. I felt like singing. I loved Virginia at that moment; the sound of hoofs on the hard track, and the lovely view of the dreaming mountains already turning red and green in places, but still romantic, wild and full of adventure. Mum has often complained that I never learn from bitter experience. She says that I'm an incurable adventurer and will come to a sticky end. I think she must be right, because I remember that at that moment I longed for an exciting chase through the mountains more than anything else, in spite of the awful things which had happened only the day before.

When we came to the mountains we parted, each taking his own trail.

"Be seeing you," we called to one another, and, "Best of luck."

My trail was one of the loveliest; the ground was soft and green, the sun shone through the trees, lighting the undergrowth with gold. Pelican's stride became long and free.

I sang loudly as I rode up and up into the mountains. I didn't feel like an exile; I felt terribly at home with the creak of leather, reins between my fingers, and Pelican's grey ears cocking backwards and forwards as he listened to my songs.

6

When I reached my turning point, I had already passed several cattle. The sun was much hotter and Pelican was sweating. I hoped that Angus wasn't too hot in the hospital; then I remembered that I was in America and every hospital was sure to have air-conditioning. I was sorry that he was missing the round-up, because it's the sort of thing he loves. I imagined him in a very clean bed eating grapes and reading magazines.

Pelican was pleased to turn round and start back down the trail. We made several detours to collect cattle and soon we had a herd of five or six in front of us. Pelican was marvellous. He plunged willingly into the most awful clumps of brambles and was far handier than I had expected. I felt like a real cowboy as my herd gradually grew; I decided that some day I would take a job on a ranch and round up cattle from dawn to dusk. Later I was to learn that Jeeps have replaced horses to a large extent in the Wild West, and that being a cowboy is terribly exhausting, particularly in winter. But now, as my herd grew and grew, I was happy with my illusions and I whistled cheerfully as I rode down towards the valley.

And then, quite suddenly, I heard hoofs. At first I thought it must be one of the Millers coming for help. Then a neigh echoed through the mountains and three horses came jumping the undergrowth – the bay mare, Easter and our phantom horse the palomino. Pelican threw up his head. The cattle stopped. Time seemed to stand still. Easter's saddle was half under his stomach; his martingale was dangling; his bridle had disappeared. They snorted when they saw the cattle, and sniffed the air. Easter looked peculiar without his bridle – like a person who wears spectacles suddenly appearing without them.

Pelican whinnied and the three horses advanced slowly. I held my breath. I could hear Phil calling to his cattle in the valley. A grey squirrel crossed the trail. My herd started to move. The three horses looked at Pelican; they skirted the cattle and began to walk on towards the valley. I felt like cheering them. I now had a herd of cattle and three horses. If only they'd remain quiet and calm when we reached the open, I might have a chance, I decided. The palomino looked wonderful, leading us all. The sun shone on his gold coat, flaxen mane and tail; he walked with a long, effortless stride. The other horses had to jog to keep up with him and the cattle ambled behind, bellowing and mooing at intervals. I felt very happy and triumphant. I knew no one else could have collected a herd like mine, and the vicious Pelican was behaving beautifully.

We reached the valley and I saw other herds approaching the allotted field. I could see that Pete and I were destined to meet quite soon. Everyone started to shout and cheer when they saw me. The palomino, Easter and the bay mare threw up their heads and I started to hurry the cattle. I didn't want to lose them, now that we were so near the field; most of all I didn't want to lose the three horses. Wendy was coming round the corner of the valley; her herd looked enormous with at least half a dozen young heifers, as well as young bulls, cows and calves. Mr and Mrs Miller, Joe and George were spread out by the field gate. The palomino broke into a canter, Easter and the bay mare followed. The cattle started to run awkwardly after them.

"Take them slowly," I heard Pete call. "You'll never get them in that way."

Then, quite suddenly, my herd was out of control. The palomino was leading it away from the gate and the people waiting in the valley.

The three horses were galloping in front, their manes and tails flying, their hoofs leaving a trail of dust behind them. I knew I had to turn them. It was no good Pete yelling, "Take them slowly." A few more minutes dallying and my herd would be lost. I pushed Pelican into a gallop, and there was dust in my eyes and my mouth; it stuck to my face and shirt, to Pelican's grey coat. It was everywhere and in the midst of it were my cattle galloping madly in pursuit of the three horses.

I urged Pelican faster. His ears were back; he felt as though years had passed since he had last been asked to gallop. But he did his best, and soon we had passed the cattle and were gaining steadily on Easter. The palomino was outstripping us all.

Then from another direction came Phil. His dun mare was dark with sweat; he carried a hunting whip and he was yelling, "Back, back. Get back."

I hoped he didn't mean me. I had no intention of turning back at that moment. I urged Pelican faster. I thought how lovely the palomino looked, and wondered whether he would look the same when he wasn't wild any more, when Angus and I had him standing in the stable at Mountain Farm. I was alongside Easter now. We had reached the low-lying land. I passed Easter; the ground was squelchy under

Pelican's hoofs and I could hear the frogs singing endlessly. The cattle were no longer with us. Instead of dust, there was mud in my face, and flying stones. Phil was gaining; another moment and he was in front of the palomino. The horses turned and I turned too, almost colliding with Phil.

"Great work," he cried. "We'll have the darned horse yet."

Now we were galloping towards the gate and the waiting people. Pete had collected my cattle, making one gigantic herd. Wendy was moving slowly across the valley. I wondered who would have the wild horse if we caught him now. I didn't want to share him with the Millers. I wanted to have a horse of our own looking out of the loose boxes at Mountain Farm.

Easter was already giving in. We had to keep driving him, otherwise he would have been trotting on his own behind the others.

As we drew near the gate, Wendy and Pete left their herds to come to our assistance. Poor Pelican was nearly finished; he was almost gasping for breath.

"Let them come in slowly. Gently does it," Mr Miller called.

We were nearly there. Phil's herd was already in the paddock. Charlie and Joe were smiling and gesticulating with large sticks.

The bay mare and Easter broke into a trot.

They looked exhausted; Easter's saddle was plastered with mud, his stirrups and leathers were missing.

"Boy, if only we can get them all in," Wendy shouted.

Pete's face was grim and determined.

"Come on now, let's see what you can do," Charlie called.

The palomino was eyeing the gate warily, and now no one spoke. The vital moment had come. The three horses all slowed to a walk. Pete, Phil, Wendy and I edged closer. Back in the valley, Pete's herd was slowly returning to the mountains.

We moved forward cautiously, and quite suddenly the bay mare took the lead and walked fearlessly into the paddock; Easter followed. We waited in silence for the palomino to follow. He stopped and gazed at the landscape; he stood very erect and sniffed the air. My heart seemed to stand still. Another moment and he might be ours. And then he made up his mind. He turned on his hocks and faced us, and Phil cried, "Get back, will you. Get back," and cracked his whip. The men rushed forward with their sticks.

Wendy screamed, "Quick. Do something," though who she was addressing no one knew.

The palomino ignored the cracking whip. He ran straight for the two men waving sticks; he lengthened his stride, took off and jumped over

Joe with tremendous scope; another second and he was galloping away towards the mountains and freedom.

Mr Miller slammed the field gate. "Well, of all the doggone horses . . . !" he exclaimed. "One can't help liking him though."

"I think he's heavenly," Mrs Miller said.

George and Joe were talking together. I dismounted and loosened Pelican's girth. Somehow, everything seemed flat.

"I don't believe we'll ever catch him," Wendy said.

"You were marvellous, Jean. I never knew the old horse had it in him," Mr Miller told me, patting Pelican.

"No one can give him a bad name any more," Wendy said.

I could see Mrs Miller laughing. "I don't know what you look like, Jean," she said.

"What about the rest of the cattle?" Pete asked.

"They'll be back in the mountains by now," Mr Miller replied.

"Well, my mare's had more than enough," Phil said, patting the dun's neck.

"Poor old Sally's nearly all in. She was great though," Wendy told me, kissing Sally's nose.

"Let's break off until after lunch anyway," Mr Miller suggested. "I guess we've all had enough."

We took the horses back to the stable. Joe appeared with Easter and said, "The saddle's all broke up. And he's lost his bridle altogether."

I felt horribly guilty. I felt Pete looking at me.

"Never mind. Let's forget it," he said.

"I'm sorry. I'm really terribly sorry," I apologised. I didn't know what else to say. I couldn't offer to buy another one because I hadn't any dollars.

"Don't worry, Jean. It doesn't matter at all.

We've got dozens of saddles just rotting in the tack room," Wendy told me.

"If you never spoil another saddle, Jean, you'll be doing all right," Phil added.

"There's the bridle, too," I replied, taking off Pelican's tack.

"It was only an old one made up of scraps. He's got his own special show one. So do stop worrying, Jean," Wendy said.

We turned out the horses so that they could roll and cool off slowly.

"If we were posh we'd slosh them down and get going with sweat scrapers. But it's too much trouble," Wendy told me.

We wandered indoors and ate large helpings of ice cream from one of the freezers.

"You never caught the wild horse, then?" Annie asked, and then she started chasing Phil round the kitchen table because he had spilt ice cream on the floor. Mrs Miller came in and said that we shouldn't be eating ice cream just before lunch, and told us all to wash our hands and faces.

After we had tidied ourselves up, Wendy and I laid the dining-room table. There was cold rib roast, pineapple salad, corn, hot rolls and apple-sauce for lunch. After we had finished eating, we caught the horses and gave them feeds. Pete and Phil disappeared to help with the harvest, and Wendy and I spent the afternoon playing with the dogs and looking at Wendy's books. We didn't have tea, but at five o'clock Phil and Pete returned and we all drank Cokes and ate chocolate, bread and cheese, and some cookies which Annie had just made.

"A few more days and we'll be through," Pete said, referring to the harvest.

"And I shan't be sorry," Phil replied.

"I wish Dad would let me drive one of the tractors. He knows I can," Wendy said.

"I'm going to fetch the rest of the cattle in now. Anyone like to help?" Pete asked.

"I'll open the gate for you when they're down off the mountains," Phil replied. "But I'm darned if I'm doing any more riding today."

"I'm going to read. I'm not halfway through the book Miss Saunders gave me to read during the vacation, and school starts in another two or three weeks," Wendy replied.

In spite of the exciting morning I wasn't at all tired. "I'd like to help," I said.

"That's fine. There's no one I would rather have," Pete replied, his grey eyes looking at me seriously.

"But who shall I ride? I'm sure Pelican's had enough," I said.

"You're welcome to my mare. She can go all day and she's still game at the end," Phil told me.

I thanked Phil, and then Pete and I collected

tack from the saddle room. The dun mare was very sweet. She sniffed me all over and lowered her head so that I could put her bridle on. Pete gave me a leg up and then we set off together across the valley.

Evening was in the air, and the mountains looked very remote and blue in the gathering dusk. I admired the landscape, and Pete said, "One day we must take you for a moonlight ride. That's really something. And you must come hunting."

"That'll be lovely," I replied.

"I wish we could catch that darned horse this evening," Pete said. "I don't want to share him with Phil and Wendy, because we'd be fighting all the time. But I wouldn't mind going halves with you."

I felt stupidly embarrassed. I didn't like to explain that I wanted the horse to be Angus's and mine and no one else's. It would sound unfriendly, particularly when the Millers had been so terribly kind to us. In the end I said nothing, and we rode round the mountains in silence, and then took a trail which I had never seen before.

I felt very high up on the dun mare. I think she was the tallest horse I had ever ridden. She carried her head rather too high and her stride was a bit short for a horse of nearly sixteen hands.

We collected cattle as we rode. Pete seemed an old hand at rounding up. Soon we had a herd of twelve or more and we turned for home, taking a trail which I recognised. I told Pete how I wished to be a cowboy and he laughed and told me about the Jeeps and the cold winters out West. "Never mind, Jean, you can come and stay at my farm whenever you like and round up my cattle from dawn to dark," he said.

"That'll be super. Thank you very much," I replied. But I still wanted to live on a ranch with covered wagons, and long trips into the West, and campfires. I shall just go on searching till I find a real ranch, I decided.

The sun was setting as we came to the valley. Behind the mountains the sky was red and gold. I felt like a character in a book or a film as I looked at our herd, and the dun's long neck and large ears, and the Millers' white house with its windows lit up, and its pillars and the lake in front.

We should have lassoes, I thought, and revolvers in holsters. We're not really dressed for the occasion. And our saddles were wrong too. Pete was whistling a tune I had never heard before. The dun mare walked with a swing. My life in England seemed far away and infinitely remote. Wendy and Phil were waiting by the field gate, whistling, talking and chewing grass.

They didn't seem so tall now that I knew them better, though I still felt tiny whenever I stood beside them.

"Looks as though you've got them all, Pete," Phil bawled.

The cattle weren't giving us much trouble, though they dodged a bit when they came to the gate. Then one of the calves separated from his mother and they both panicked. It took us nearly twenty minutes to get them together again.

It was quite dark when Pete and I rode round to the stable yard. The other horses had all been turned out.

"Did you enjoy it?" Pete asked.

"Yes, like anything. It was really great," I replied.

"I expect your brother will be okay tomorrow, and you'll be going back to Mountain Farm. We've really enjoyed having you here. I just wanted to tell you that," Pete said, taking off his chestnut's saddle.

"It's been super. I've loved staying here," I replied, and I realised suddenly how difficult tomorrow would be.

I should have to face my parents and they doubtless would be furious with the way Angus and I had behaved. I knew we had no excuse to offer; we had deliberately disobeyed every instruction they had given us, at least that's the way they would see it, and it would be mostly true. I didn't think we would be able to make them realise how completely we had lost our heads when we had seen the palomino and the bay mare. They'd never understand, and anyway it was inexcusable not to turn back later when we had remembered. I expect we won't be allowed to ride for ages and ages, I thought gloomily, and I saw us hanging around Mountain Farm day after day with absolutely nothing to do.

We fed the horses and put the tack away. "It's been a lovely day, I've enjoyed every moment of it. It's really been one of the niceest days I've ever spent," I told Pete as we walked up to the house together.

"I've enjoyed it too," he said.

Supper was waiting for us. The dining-room table was lit by candlelight. We ate freshwater fish cooked in wine, asparagus, hot rolls and peaches and ice cream. I felt quite sick when eventually I stopped eating.

"Your father rang up. He'll be fetching you before he goes to Washington in the morning," Mr Miller told me.

"Right. I'll be ready. How's Angus?" I asked.

"Fine. Full of life," Mr Miller replied. "There's not a scratch on him."

After supper we all helped wash up; then Pete and I wandered down to the stable and turned out the two horses we had ridden.

Wendy and I went to bed soon after that. The night was terribly warm and I didn't sleep for hours. The moon rose round and red and shone on our two beds; the frogs sang incessantly; rooks cawed raucously and circled the large trees beyond the lawn. I thought of Angus in the hospital, of Mountain Farm empty, dreaming in the moonlight, of the friends I had left behind in England. I hoped that Moonlight and Mermaid were happy, and then, at last, I slept.

7

I got up very early. I wanted to say goodbye to all the animals before I left. I had an idea it would be ages before I was allowed to see the Millers' house again.

George and Joe were milking the house cows. They asked after Angus and let me try my hand at milking. They were very pleased that Angus wasn't hurt. I had never seen a cow milked by hand before and I wasn't much good at it. I wandered back to the house and met Pete. "You get earlier and earlier," he said.

We fed the horses together and Pete asked whether I would like to take Easter and the bay mare back to Mountain Farm. I said that I'd better ask my parents first.

I hardly ate any breakfast because of being sad about leaving. When I had finished I said goodbye to Annie, and then I heard Dad hooting impatiently outside the front door. I rushed into the dining-room, where the Millers were still eating, and shouted goodbye to everyone. I kissed Cop, and rushing outside I ran straight into a pillar.

Dad said, "Do look where you're going. Have you hurt yourself? We don't want any more accidents."

I rubbed my head. "No, I'm okay," I said, but I hit my head again as I got into the car.

"You seem determined to do yourself in," Dad remarked.

I felt cross. "How's Angus?" I asked.

"Completely recovered," Dad replied.

I waited for him to ask how we came to be in the mountains. But he didn't. We drove away from the Millers' house, down the long drive, in silence.

Mountain Farm looked very small. The yard seemed tiny. Dad said, "I'll just drop you and drive on. I'm late already."

Angus was waiting by the front door. "Hello," he called.

He looked marvellous, but tiny after Phil and Pete. "I only had concussion," he said. "The hospital was awful; they kept me in a darkened room and there was absolutely nothing to do."

Angus and I wandered round to the stable after I had seen Mum. "You know we're not to ride again for the whole holidays, don't you?" he asked. I felt a huge lump rising in my throat. "I told them everything. What else could I do?" he asked.

"Of course. You couldn't do anything else," I said.

"It sounded so awful when I started to explain. Not at all like it really was. I expect you could have told them better," Angus said. "They were nice about it really. I mean I suppose we had to have some sort of punishment, I expect if we had children, we'd do just the same."

"You mean about punishing them?" I asked. "Personally, I'd much rather be smacked or made to write *I must do what my parents tell me* five hundred times. Wouldn't you?"

"Much. But the point is they wanted to choose the worst punishment they could think of," Angus said.

"Well, they've certainly succeeded," I replied. I saw the rest of the holidays stretching before us, long sunny days, beautiful early mornings. I saw the mountains calling us, their trails waiting to be explored. And we'll be stuck here, I thought, with no horses to ride. We'll see the Millers riding past, horses grazing in the valley, and we'll know that till term starts we can't ride anywhere, not even to the end of the dirt road and back. "We'll never catch the wild horse now," I said.

"Well, it's our own fault. We can't blame anyone else. It's no good being cross. We'll just have to make the best of it," Angus replied.

"Can we walk where we like?" I asked.

"Not off the property for a week," Angus replied.

"We may as well commit suicide," I said.

"Don't be so hysterical. What's a week or a month? A mere drop in the ocean of our lives," Angus replied.

I could see that my brother had been considering our punishment for some time and was now determined to make the best of it. I started to tell him about my stay with the Millers.

"They were all incredibly nice; though I think I like Pete best," I finished.

"And what did you do with the chocolates?" Angus asked.

"Ate them of course. I've still got the pen though," I replied.

"You might have kept some for your poor sick brother," Angus said.

"I decided that you probably had piles of grapes and peaches. Sick people always get masses to eat," I replied.

We wandered into the house and out again. There seemed absolutely nothing to do. Mum told us to tidy our bedrooms, which she said were like pigsties. I began to dread the next week.

"We'll have to write poetry or something," Angus said in desperation.

After lunch Pete rang up. He wanted to know whether we'd like some horses brought over. I explained about our punishment and he said, "Tough luck. Never mind, if you can't come to us, we'll come to you. We've got two-thirds of the harvest in. There's nothing to stop us bringing sandwiches and spending the whole darned day with you. So cheer up, we'll come right over tomorrow, Jean."

I said, "That'll be great. But remember we can't ride. What will you do all day?"

"Plenty. I've got all sorts of ideas," Pete replied. "Be seeing you."

I told Angus what Pete had said. He looked worried. "I can't see what the heck they'll do here all day," he said. "They're not the sort of people who can sit about and read for hours."

"Well, it's no good worrying. I've told them how the land lies," I replied.

We spent the afternoon reading books. We told Mum about the Millers' impending visit, and she said, "I can't imagine what they'll do all day. I should think they'd be bored to tears."

The paddock and the stable looked horribly empty without any horses. The evening dragged slowly on till bedtime.

I woke up the next morning filled with trepidation. I was certain Mum was right – the Millers would be bored to tears. I pictured them yawning and looking at their watches. I wished that they hadn't decided to visit us. Angus felt the same. We both appeared for breakfast with dismal faces.

It was another perfect day. "If only we had a swimming-pool," Angus said.

"Or a tennis court, or even a swing," I added.

"I'm glad you haven't either. You're dangerous enough as it is," Mum said.

"I can't see that there's anything dangerous in a swing," Angus replied.

"Can't you?" Mum answered. "For one thing, you'd probably knock each other's eyes out with the corners, or go so high that you'd become entangled with a tree."

I was furious that Mum could think we'd be so silly. I'd often played with swings before. It was maddening not to be trusted at all. One day we'll show Mum and Dad what we're really like, I thought.

The Millers arrived in the Jeep at ten o'clock. Phil was driving. Apparently, you can have a licence at fifteen in most states as long as your parents agree.

"We've brought some paint. We thought we'd start on the inside of the stable," Wendy yelled.

"Great idea," Angus said.

Phil drove the Jeep into the yard and we all helped pull out brushes and tins of emulsion.

"We wanted to bring a couple of the men

along to help some. But the old man wasn't agreeable," Pete told us.

"I'm starting on the cobwebs. Do you think you could get the long brush out of the kitchen for me, Angus?" Wendy asked.

"I expect we'll have to brush down the walls first," Pete said.

We spent the entire day painting the stable. Wendy broke the brush she was using and

insisted on going indoors to apologise to Mum. Phil cracked jokes all the time. The Millers wouldn't come in for lunch. They said they'd only upset our parents, and anyway they weren't suitably dressed.

By the time the Millers left the stable looked marvellous. They had to return the Jeep by six o'clock, when the men would need it to take them home. Before they drove away I thanked them all again for having me. They said silly things like "Darned generous of us" and "Can't think why we did."

Angus and I watched the Jeep disappearing along the dirt road. "You can't say today's been dull," Angus said.

"Far from it," I agreed.

The next few days were terribly dull. I wrote some very bad poetry; Angus made two saddle-racks to hang in the stable. Mum bought us a pot of paint and we painted the loose box doors dark green.

We spent one afternoon visiting our new school. Mr Miller came with us and Mum and Dad, and introduced us to the headmaster. It was a school for boys as well as girls; Pete and Phil had just left it for a military academy; Wendy would be leaving after Christmas. There was a baseball pitch, and the buildings were low, modern and rambling. The headmaster, Mr Beeton, was tall, with narrow shoulders and fair hair. He gave us all tea in his small, two-storey, brick house. He was not at all frightening, and talked to Angus and me as though we were grown-ups. We discovered that our education was in advance of American children of our age. Mum and Dad seemed well pleased with the school, and Mr Beeton. And we thought it very nice of him to give us tea, which is not a usual American meal.

Before Pete and Phil left for the military academy they brought back the bay mare and Frances to Mountain Farm. We were all very sad now that the summer holidays were over; and we hadn't managed to catch the wild horse. The weather was still marvellous; the mountains had become a mass of greens, browns and oranges; there was a feeling of autumn, what the Millers called the fall, in the air.

Phil and Pete said goodbye on a misty morning. They looked very dashing in their uniforms. They had gleaming white belts, and every buckle and button on their tunics was shining.

We stood together in the yard and Phil said, "It's not long before we'll be back again and then we really will catch that darned horse."

"If you haven't caught him already," Pete added.

"You'll be pretty smart if you do," Phil said, using smart in the American sense when it means clever, cunning or sharp, or really a mixture of all three.

"I don't think we will," Wendy replied.

"We're jolly well going to try, anyway," Angus said.

Pete kicked a stone and we stood and said nothing, while the mist cleared from the mountains and the sun shone on the valley.

"I hope you get on all right at school, Jean. I guess you may find it kind of rough after life in England," Pete told me.

"I'll look after her all right," Wendy said.

"She's champion wrestler in the school and captain of the baseball team," Phil told us.

Pete and Phil left at last and when they had gone the holidays seemed really over.

Tomorrow was to be our first day at school in America.

8

On an October evening when Angus and I had finished riding and were just starting our homework, Wendy telephoned. I answered and she came to the point straight away.

"I say, Jean, we've just realised it's the opening meet of the Jameson hounds next Saturday, and we just wondered whether you and Angus would like to come along with us," she said.

The Jameson hunt is one of the smartest packs in Virginia. The subscription is something like a thousand pounds. I wondered what the cap would be.

"We'd love to. But I shall have to ask Mum and Dad. Is the meet near? I mean, can we hack?" I asked.

"Don't be dumb. Your horses can travel with mine in the truck," Wendy replied.

"Thanks a million. Hang on," I said.

Mum was reading. Dad was writing letters. It was a bad moment to ask a favour. "It's Wendy," I said. "She wants to know whether we can go to the opening meet with her on Saturday."

Angus had listened to the telephone conversation on the other phone. "She will take our horses with hers in their truck," he added.

"What's the cap?" Dad asked. "How much will you have to pay?"

"Who'll look after you?" Mum inquired.

"Why do we need looking after? We hunted on our own in England," Angus said.

I could hear Wendy's voice coming from the receiver in the hall.

"I forgot to ask," I replied.

"You'd better find out then," Dad told me.

I rushed back to the telephone. I suddenly wanted to hunt terribly badly. "Hello," I said. "Dad wants to know who'll look after us, and what's the cap?"

"Heavens above, you're not kids of six!" Wendy said, and I thought there was a scorn in her voice. "Dad will be following in the station wagon and you'll be our guests, so there won't be any caps."

"Thanks awfully. It's terribly nice of you," I replied.

"Oh, forget it," she said, sounding bored. I imagined her thinking: Molly-coddled English children! Wendy can be very scornful.

I rushed back to my parents and gabbled, "There's no cap to pay. Mr Miller will look after us."

Dad said, "Do speak more slowly."

I repeated what I had said, adding that we were to be the Millers' guests for the day.

"I must say that's very good of Charlie," Dad remarked.

I could still hear Wendy's voice in the hall. I thought: In another moment she'll be fed up and ring off.

I said, "She's still holding on."

Dad turned to Mum and said, "What do you think, Angela?" in that maddeningly slow way parents sometimes have when you're in a hurry.

"I don't see why they shouldn't go, if only they can be sensible," Mum replied.

I rushed to the telephone. "Yes, we can go. Thank you so much," I cried.

"Hurray, that's great. See you tomorrow at school," Wendy said.

I felt quite limp when I had put down the receiver. I had never imagined that we should hunt – not in my wildest dreams, and certainly not with the Jameson hounds. I stood by the telephone for a moment, seeing hounds drawing a tiny covert, myself riding Frances, Angus well mounted on the bay mare. Oh, we are lucky, I thought. To think that we're really going to hunt in America.

Angus was overjoyed. Only our parents were dubious.

"Remember it's better to go round a fence than to risk a broken neck," Dad warned.

"We really will try to be sensible," Angus replied, and he sounded as though he really meant it.

I remembered the last time he had promised the same thing. And this time he really will, I told myself.

For the rest of the evening Angus and I could think of nothing but hunting. The next morning we rose early and groomed the ponies for hours. We collected information about the Jameson hounds at school. We discovered that they belonged to a very rich family called the Smythes and had been started in 1908. We also discovered that the Smythes were the owners of the wild horse.

Wendy told us that we must bring our horses over to the Millers' place by ten o'clock. The meet was quite close, but no one seemed to consider hacking.

Angus and I spent a great deal of time sponging and pressing our riding-clothes. We could think of nothing but the meet and we increased our horses' oats and corn by several double handfuls and ears. Our parents decided to attend the meet. They also invited people to stay for the weekend.

The weather stayed warm. Thursday arrived and we found that Frances had a loose shoe. A terrible search for a blacksmith ensued. At last we heard of one, who came in an enormous pick-up truck and shod Frances at seven o'clock in the evening.

Friday was warm but there were a few scattered showers. I was kept in after school because I hadn't attended to a history lesson. Angus was furious, and he, Wendy and Mr Miller had to wait for me. And though they were all very nice about it, I felt horribly guilty.

Angus and I rode for about twenty minutes when at last we reached home. Then we cleaned the tack, which wasn't very dirty. We groomed the ponies until it was dark, and gave them three ears of corn each and a large feed of oats.

"I hope they won't be too fresh," Angus said. "I wish we were hacking to the meet."

"What sandwiches would you like? Ham, egg or cheese?" Mum asked, when we entered the kitchen.

"Ham, please," we both answered.

It seemed funny to be preparing for hunting again. Particularly so far from home. I couldn't believe that we would ever really arrive at the meet. It all seemed a little too good to be true.

Angus charged about the house collecting his clothes and singing "John Peel". Mum gave us lots of advice; I decided that we must get up at six, have mucked out by six-thirty and have the horses ready by nine. Angus said I was mad and if we got up at seven we would still have plenty of time. In the end we agreed to split the difference and set the alarm clock for six-thirty.

I don't think I slept much that night. I was terribly excited, and a little apprehensive because I knew that neither the bay mare nor Frances had hunted before. I was determined that Angus and I would behave sensibly – I dreaded another accident – but would our mounts be sensible, I wondered, tossing and turning in bed. I could see the bay mare in my imagination, kicking other members of the field, cantering sideways, barging into horses with her quarters. Frances, I decided, would probably buck. I saw myself falling off in front of the entire field. In more optimistic moments I saw both our horses behaving beautifully, and us patting them enthusiastically at the end of the best run for many seasons. I dreamed about school when I finally fell asleep. Angus and I were playing baseball and then suddenly the baseball bat became a hunting-horn and we were running madly across fields in pursuit of hounds. I wakened to the shrill ring of the alarm clock.

The morning was warm and still. I shouted at Angus, washed and dressed quickly and rushed down to the stable. Frances was lying down. The bay mare was gazing over her door at the new day. I gave them both water and a little hay. Frances was very dirty and I had to fetch hot water and soap from the kitchen. Angus appeared still half asleep.

"Thank goodness my mount's bay," he said.

I washed Frances. The sky turned blue; the sun shone. It was like a warm March day in England.

"I'm afraid it's going to be too bright for much scent," Angus said.

We mucked out the boxes and then dashed indoors and gobbled a breakfast of scrambled eggs on toast.

We had decided to plait the horses' manes. I had two reels of thread for Frances, one chestnut, one white. We groomed the horses first and then we plaited, which took ages. Frances had a thin wispy mane. The bay mare's was thick. I sewed some plaits three times and they still looked awful, and then it was too late to resew any of them. By this time the bay mare had six enormously fat plaits and a forelock; Frances had seven thin ones and lots of wispy hair which had refused to become plaits. We gave the horses feeds and hurried indoors. By now it was ten to nine.

"We mustn't be late at the Millers'," Angus said.

Angus and I bridled our mounts at half past nine. Our pockets were stuffed with sandwiches. We mounted and rode across the valley. Frances felt fresh; the bay mare jogged and wouldn't walk. We could see our parents waving by the back door.

"Well at least we aren't late so far," Angus said cheerfully.

Wendy was waiting for us in the stable yard. She was dressed in light-coloured breeches, a black coat, a hunting-tie and black boots. She wore a bowler and carried an extremely elegant hunting-whip. Suddenly, our clothes seemed all wrong and rather shabby. Her hair was neatly tucked into a net; her clothes looked almost new. Somehow I hadn't expected Wendy to be smart. Normally she would ride in anything – worn jeans and sneakers; tattered breeches and decrepit Newmarket boots. A flying jacket, a leather waistcoat, a colossal jersey, moccasins and old slacks and a checked shirt. I was speechless for a moment. So was Angus.

"Hi, you're in fine time. The truck's out in front," Wendy said.

"You look very smart. Really great," Angus exclaimed.

"I feel awful. I'm sure my coat doesn't fit. It was Mum's," she replied.

"Does it matter that we're wearing riding-hats?" I asked. "You see, we haven't got bowlers."

"Of course not. Everybody will think you're about ten anyway," Wendy answered with a grin.

"I don't think that's much of a compliment," Angus said.

Although Wendy had said "truck" from the beginning, I was surprised to see Pete's chestnut standing in an open truck. I had imagined a horse box. The truck looked small for three horses.

"What's the matter? Don't you like our transport?" Wendy asked.

I could see Angus looking at the three rails which served for sides. I saw that there was no ramp.

"How do we get them in?" I inquired.

"Just by leading. How the heck do you think? That's why the truck's against the hill. We have got a loading ramp which we drive the cattle down, but we find the horses like jumping in off the hill a whole lot more," Wendy replied, leading the way towards the truck.

I was glad Mum hadn't seen our form of transport.

Pete's chestnut was wearing a rug. His mane wasn't plaited, but I saw that he had been clipped. Joe was by the truck and he grinned and waved when he saw us. "He's coming too," Wendy said.

Angus looked at the chestnut. "I feel very scruffy, don't you, Jean?" he whispered. "Wendy's so smart. Do you think everyone else will be?"

"I expect so, but it doesn't really matter," I answered without conviction.

"I can't think why we didn't have the horses clipped," Angus said.

"It would have been awfully difficult and we would have had to buy the rugs," I replied.

"I wish we were rich. It didn't seem to matter in England, but it does here," Angus said.

"You mean us never having enough money?" I asked. "You can't say we're poor with Dad's job."

"But he isn't paid a million dollars a year."

"Do stop grumbling," I said. "We're very lucky to be going hunting at all."

Joe took Frances and, after a little persuasion, she jumped into the truck. He tied her to one of the rails by her reins, which made Angus raise his eyebrows. The bay mare was more difficult. She ran backwards and reared and oats had to be fetched. Mr Miller appeared on the scene and everyone started to give each other instructions. Mrs Miller appeared and took photographs, which didn't seem to help much. Then, quite suddenly, the bay mare decided to be sensible and jumped calmly into the truck, and stood still beside Frances. Mr Miller cheered.

Joe tied her to the rails by her reins and then he climbed into the cab. Wendy, Angus and I climbed in with the horses, though Mrs Miller seemed nervous and thought we would be better in the front with Joe.

We waved madly as Joe drove the truck down the hill. I must say it didn't feel at all safe. The floorboards seemed loose and the rails at the sides were only fastened by a few nails. I hoped we wouldn't meet Mum and Dad before we reached our destination. The horses were restless, and I untied Frances because I didn't want her to break her reins before we reached the meet.

Soon we were travelling along the highway; air rushed at our faces and once Angus nearly lost his hat. Wendy started to tell us about the Master of the Jameson hounds.

"He's madly handsome and has a sweet wife. He hunts hounds himself and he's really great

on a horse. He's strict though, so be careful," she warned us.

I imagined a tall, slim figure in pink sitting astride an enormous well-bred hunter. He'll look disdainfully at our hacking-jackets, I thought, gloomily, and he'll send us home when he sees our riding-hats.

"He's terribly nice though," Wendy added as an afterthought.

9

The meet was outside a large, low, rambling white house. In front was a sweep of gravel, behind were the stables where we unloaded our horses on to a manure heap, there being no loading ramp or hill nearby. The stables were marvellous: built in a square, painted white with a veranda running round the entire yard, they were quite unlike anything I had seen before. Inside the buildings, the boxes were partly tiled and the saddle rooms were magnificently arranged with marvellous sinks and elegantly tiled floors. Grooms were rushing backwards and forwards with tack and stable rubbers and tins of hoof oil.

"Isn't it all super!" Angus exclaimed.

I was looking at other horses' plaits. I thought ours looked amateurish in comparison.

"Let's go. I hope Dad's here," Wendy said. She seemed nervous and ill at ease now that we had arrived. "I hope the horses behave," she added.

Joe held our stirrups while we mounted. Frances napped towards the bay mare. We rode round to the front of the house.

There wasn't a large field by English standards. An elegant maid in uniform was offering coffee to the twenty or thirty assembled horsemen, and to the spectators who had arrived in cars. There were plenty of grooms; but no interested locals like one sees at English meets. It was very much a class affair, and nearly all the horsemen were marvellously turned out in scarlet and toppers. There was one woman riding sidesaddle, who had blue-rinsed hair which she wore in a bun under a top hat. Another woman wore a coat with swallow-tails. There was only one rider in rat-catcher besides ourselves, and she was an English girl of about eighteen.

Hounds looked marvellous and all very much of a size. The Master rode a large chestnut. The one whipper-in was mounted on a bay. Wendy nodded to one or two people; then Mr Miller appeared and said, "You'd better meet Mr Smythe, the Master."

There was no sign of Mum and Dad.

We followed Mr Miller across the drive and he introduced us to Mr Smythe as "Two visitors from England."

Mr Smythe smiled and said, "I hope we give you a good day."

Angus said, "Thank you, sir."

Then Frances started to run backwards into hounds and we hastily retreated.

"It's not nearly as friendly as an English meet," Angus complained.

"It's probably only because we're strangers," I said. But I thought of meets at home in England. I remembered the crowds outside a country pub, mothers with push-chairs, children on bicycles, old-age pensioners, young men on motor-bikes, shabby foot followers. Everyone in the village would be there and everyone would know everyone else. There would be a fleet of cars and bicycles and foot followers behind the field when we set off to draw the first covert. There would be cameras clicking and a great feeling of comradeship. Here, in America, the sport seemed to belong only to a selected few. There was something missing, I thought, watching the maid hand Mr Miller a cup of coffee.

"There's Mum," Angus said.

Our parents had arrived with their weekend guests. Dad came across to where we stood.

"Where's Mr Miller? I thought he was going to look after you," he said.

I suddenly had an awful empty feeling in the pit of my stomach. It was obvious that Dad expected Mr Miller to be mounted. It's funny how we just can't do anything right, I thought.

"He's over there," Angus replied, pointing to where Mr Miller stood talking to a fat man who was mounted on a small bay horse.

"But he's not even dressed for riding. How can he look after you without a horse?" Dad asked.

Then Mum appeared. "Where's Charlie?" she inquired.

"He's following in the station wagon. He always does," I replied.

"I don't see how he can look after you when he's in a car," Dad said.

"It doesn't sound a very good arrangement to me," Mum said.

"I suppose we can't do anything about it now," Dad told us, "but I wish you had explained the situation to us before."

"We didn't really think about it," I replied truthfully. "Wendy just said that he would look after us and would be following in the station wagon."

"They're just going to move off," Angus said, looking at the hounds.

"Well, do try and be sensible," Mum said.

"I'll keep an eye on them," Wendy promised.

"Remember, they don't even know the country," Dad said.

The Master blew a short toot on his horn. We rode away down the drive in bright sunlight. The sky was still blue. It was the beginning of our first hunt in America.

A crowd of second horsemen followed the

field at a respectful distance. We crossed a road and passed through an open gate into a large meadow where everyone started to canter. The bay mare bucked; Frances banged the woman with the blue hair with her quarters. Wendy said, "Don't thrust, Jean," and I felt furious because I had hunted quite often in England and didn't wish to be told elementary things by Wendy.

The first covert was a small wood. Frances was sweating when we halted and Angus was having trouble with the bay mare.

"Why the heck don't you keep away from everyone else?" Wendy asked.

I tried to move Frances, but she clung to her stable companion and the bay mare clung to the other horses.

"It's all very well for you to talk. You're on an experienced hunter," I replied.

"There's no need to get mad. I'm only trying to help," Wendy said.

Frances banged the blue-haired woman again and she cried, "For heaven's sake, keep that mare still!"

The bay mare lashed out sideways at a tall man on a large grey. Angus said, "Sorry, sir."

I realised that I wasn't enjoying my hunt much so far. The English girl in rat-catcher grinned and called, "What are they – young horses?"

Then I heard someone say, "We're going to organise a real round-up on Monday," and my mind leaped to attention.

"I hear he's as wily as a grass snake," the man on the grey replied.

"We'll take him dead if not alive," someone said and I suddenly felt quite empty, because I knew they were talking about the wild horse. I glanced at Angus and saw that he too was listening to this conversation.

"He's done too much damage already. He's quite nuts. He's got three of Sam's horses with him right now," the tall man said.

"I suppose his darned pelt will be worth a few dollars," someone said with a laugh.

"Well, let's hope it doesn't come to shooting. I don't like the idea of putting a bullet in any horse's skull," the tall man replied.

There's only tomorrow, I thought desperately, and then a hound spoke.

Another hound picked up the line. "They've found," the English girl said.

Frances started to fidget. I thought of Monday. I saw scores of riders approaching the mountains. Someone hollered. I heard the horn and suddenly I was galloping with everyone else, feeling a faint breeze in my face, hearing the "gone away" echoing across the sunlit Virginian fields. We came to a wall which Frances took in her stride; we swung left and there was a hill, and at the bottom a large line of rails. "They're too big for our horses," Angus cried, suddenly beside me.

"Perhaps someone will break them," I replied.

Wendy was in front. She seemed to have forgotten all about us. Frances settled down.

I watched the Master jump the rails without changing the pace of his hunter. Other people followed.

"They certainly jump," Angus said.

Beyond the rails was more grassland and in

the distance a wood. I didn't think the hounds spoke as much as an English pack, and the Master didn't blow his horn again. But the country was far more open, so I suppose it wasn't necessary.

A grey horse broke the rails right in the centre of the fence. Angus gave a cheer. Presently we were galloping towards the wood. Hounds checked and we saw a long line of cars coming towards us across the fields. Frances was blowing quite a bit and her long coat dripped with sweat. I dismounted and loosened her girth. Wendy came across.

"Are you okay?" she asked.

"Fine," I replied.

"Have you heard about the round-up? They're going to try and catch the wild horse on Monday. Isn't it awful?" Angus said.

"Who are they?" Wendy asked.

The stream of cars had arrived. People were getting out and hailing friends.

"Everybody here as far as I can make out," Angus replied, and there was despair in his voice.

"Are you kids all right?" Mr Miller called, looking enormous in a camel-hair coat and Newmarket boots.

"Yes, thank you," I replied. At that moment a hound spoke. I pulled up my girth and mounted. There was a sudden burst of music as the whole pack picked up the line. We heard the "gone away" as we galloped towards the wood.

"They've broken on the far side," someone said. We jumped a smallish stile and then we were in the wood. I forgot everything but the feel of Frances's stride, the rushing air in my face, the music of hounds in full cry.

We slid down a bank and jumped a stream and then we were out of the wood and in open country again. Hounds were running very fast and making very little noise. A couple of big hunters swept past Frances; in front was a wall, beyond were more huge meadows. I patted Frances and wondered how long she would stand the pace. We jumped the wall and I noticed a ditch beneath as we landed. I saw that the bay mare was over as we galloped on across grassland; in the distance a large house stood beyond a terrace gazing towards the Blue Ridge Mountains. It looked completely deserted.

"That's the place Bill Matthews built for his first wife. He had to build another for his second wife, so now it stands empty," said Wendy, suddenly beside me. I was appalled by such extravagance. The next moment Wendy was past and galloping close to a big chestnut horse, ridden by a man in scarlet.

We turned left and galloped through a gateway and across a track. Hounds were well in front of the whole field. I don't think I'd ever seen a pack run so fast before. We jumped a "coop" set in a wire fence. We passed a herd of Angus cattle. I was with the tail end of the field; Angus just behind. The scene in front was like a modern sporting print though not really English in appearance because there weren't any hedges.

The field doubled back because of wire, which enabled us to gain a little ground. The sun was still shining and I was surprised that there was any scent at all.

We came to a stream, wide and treacherous, and for a moment Frances hesitated, then we were over and galloping across grass again.

As we jumped a low flight of rails, nearly ten minutes later, I realised that Angus and I were losing ground. Slowly the pack and the field mounted on fast, fit hunters were drawing away from us. Frances was tiring; the bay mare was dark with sweat.

"Let's slow down," I shouted to Angus. "It's their first hunt after all. We don't want to spoil them for the rest of the season."

We pulled up our horses and it was awful watching the hunt disappearing into the distance. But it was some consolation to know that we were doing the right thing. "What now?" Angus asked.

"Home, I suppose," I replied.

"I wish there were more and bigger woods," Angus said.

"It's marvellous country for a fast, fit horse," I replied. We couldn't hear the pack any more. It was dismal standing together in the vast Virginian countryside without a soul in sight. There wasn't even a cow within a mile of where we stood.

"I hope you know the way home, because I don't," Angus said.

"I don't, but maybe the horses do," I replied hopefully.

"Remember they travelled to the meet by truck," Angus said. So we were lost, I realised with dismay. All Virginia seemed to stretch before us.

"Oh damn," I cried. "Why can't we ever do the right thing?"

"It's not as though we don't try," Angus retorted. I saw us returning in gathering darkness; our parents waiting, anxious and angry, scanning the landscape, imagining ghastly accidents.

"If we find the truck, we only have to wait for Wendy," I said.

"Quite – if we find the truck," Angus replied.

"Well, we must know the way we came," I cried, turning Frances.

We jumped the low flight of rails again. We rode across endless grassland, and then somewhere we went wrong. We came to a ploughed field, and we both knew that we hadn't crossed one earlier in the day.

"Damn!" I said again.

"Personally, I think it's entirely Wendy's fault. After all, she was supposed to look after us," Angus exclaimed angrily.

The ploughed earth was dry and powdery. The sun had moved considerably since morning. "I guess it's about two o'clock," I said.

We ate our sandwiches. We jumped a wall and found ourselves riding across grass again.

"Americans don't think. That's the trouble," Angus said.

"You mean that Wendy didn't think far enough to remember that we were on young horses?" I asked.

"Exactly," Angus replied.

"I suppose she'll guess that we're heading for

the truck. There's not much else we could do,"
I said.

We rode through a gateway into another
grass field. We saw a stream and a wood, but
they weren't the ones we knew. We jumped
some rails and found to our horror that we
were back in the ploughed field. An awful feeling of helplessness assailed us.

"We're just riding in circles," Angus cried
desperately.

I saw us still riding aimlessly at midnight.
Oh, why did we ever go hunting? I thought
miserably. We might have known everything
would go wrong.

"What do we do now?" asked Angus, and
there was anger as well as despair in his voice.

"Let's see what the horses think," I suggested.
I dropped Frances's reins and prayed that she
would know the way home, but she only ate
the grass which grew at the edge of the field.
There was a feeling of late afternoon which
hung heavily in the air.

"We might as well give up and die," Angus
said.

"Don't be so defeatist," I replied. "I wish we
had a compass."

"Well, we haven't, so that's that," Angus
replied.

"There's no need to be so cross," I said.

"I'm not, I'm just thinking of the row we're

going to get into when we eventually return home," Angus answered.

"Well, this time it really isn't our fault," I replied, wondering how long Wendy would keep the truck waiting for us.

"This just wouldn't happen, hunting in England. A crowd of foot followers would have set us on the right road hours ago," Angus said.

"We'd better try again," I answered.

The horses were bored now as well as tired. I think they knew that we were lost. We rode on and on, and afternoon turned to evening; and then at last we reached a road. Angus gave a feeble cheer and the horses pricked their ears.

"Which way do we turn?" Angus asked.

Neither of us had ever seen the road before, but Frances seemed to know it. She turned left in a very definite manner and Angus said, "Thank goodness someone seems to know the way."

The road was narrow. It wandered between wood fences and past a few farms standing at the end of long drives.

We started to think about the wild horse as we followed the strange road. I thought of hunting him across the vast, well-fenced and little-wooded Virginian countryside. Then I remembered the approaching round-up and all my hopes and dreams seemed to die. I remembered that the Virginians would shoot him if they couldn't catch him, and there just didn't seem any point in hoping any more.

The shadows lengthened across the unknown road and Frances stumbled with weariness.

"I'm going to dismount and walk," I told Angus. He dismounted too and we walked steadily along the road in to the gathering dusk.

"If only they weren't going to shoot him," said Angus at last.

I saw the palomino falling as the bullet hit him and heard the cries of his pursuers. Then I remembered the Virginians' renowned love of horses, the stud-farms scattered across Virginia, and I knew that the palomino had a chance.

"I don't believe they'll shoot him, not when the moment comes," I said. "They're too fond of horses. It would be different if he was old, or diseased or in pain."

"I hope you're right," Angus said.

We started to worry about Wendy. We wondered if she would be waiting for us, or would she have returned home and told everyone we were lost? Or was she still hunting across the dusky fields? We both hoped that she was still hunting or hacking home like us.

We came at last to a road which met our road at right angles, and once again Frances knew the way. It was very nearly dark by now. I thought of the tea waiting for us in Mountain Farm, of warm welcoming lights and a hot bath. Frances started to hurry. Perhaps we're getting near, I thought, peering into the dusk.

But I could see nothing familiar about the road and the trees on each side were strange to us, so was the faint outline of the valley below. The bay mare was tired. I could see it by the droop of her head and in the way she walked. The road obviously meant nothing to her. Angus and I were tired too, too tired to talk. We ought to find a telephone, I thought. I imagined ringing up Mountain Farm and Dad answering. I wondered why we hadn't thought of it before. I started looking for a house; but for ages we only passed wooden shacks with unkempt gardens.

Frances still hurried. She seemed suddenly tireless. A car passed with blazing headlights and our horses cringed and blinked. There were lights ahead which showed us a house silhouetted against the dark sky. We came to a drive and, with a sudden rush, Frances swung down it as though it was home.

"Where are you going?" yelled Angus, while I felt quite sick with disappointment. So this was where Frances had been leading us, I thought, not to Mountain Farm; nor the Millers' place, but to a strange house, standing near an unknown road. I suddenly felt twice as weary. I couldn't see how we were ever to reach home, our parents could wait all night for us and still we wouldn't arrive. It must be one of

Frances's previous homes, I thought, staring furiously at the house ahead. I could hear Angus calling to me, "Where are you going, Jean? What *are* you doing?"

"There may be a telephone," I yelled back into the darkness.

Frances hurried along the drive and turned left towards the dim outline of a building, which I guessed was the stable. A horse whinnied, and the bay mare raised her head and answered. The stable was in darkness. We could just see three heads gazing at us over doors as we turned towards the house. There were lights in the kitchen and a woman opened the back door when we knocked. I explained our plight and she disappeared in search of someone.

"What are you going to do if they won't let us?" Angus asked.

"Find out where we are," I replied.

The woman returned with a lean little man in riding-clothes and a checked waistcoat.

He said, "Hi!" and then, "Gee, if it isn't Frances."

"We're trying to get home. She brought us here," I explained.

"I traded her with Charlie Miller over the other side – must be three years ago now," he said. "I traded her for the heck of a horse."

"Please may we use your phone?" I asked.

"He jumped real good, that horse. I sold him to a dealer in New York. I can't remember his name right now. Sure, you can use the phone," he added, as though he'd only just thought of it. "Do come inside."

The walls were hung with photographs of horses. There was a collection of hunting-whips and polo sticks in the hall. The house smelled of cooking, leather and saddle soap.

The telephone was in a small front room where there were whisky and beer bottles and a dozen or more glasses and tumblers. There were magazines and a couple of books on riding lying on the table in the centre of the room.

Fortunately, I knew the number of Mountain Farm. But before I could ring, the owner of the house talked. He wanted to know where we came from, which pack we'd been hunting with, how we'd come by Frances. He told me that we were roughly fifteen miles from Mountain Farm, that we'd better leave the horses with him and be fetched by car, and that his name was Jim Blackburn, and that his parents were Irish. Then he left the room and I used the phone.

I said, "It's Jean here. I'm terribly sorry, we got lost. We're fifteen miles from home and the horses are very tired. We don't know where Wendy is."

"Thank goodness you've rung up. Wendy's just got back. We were just about to send out a search-party. Where exactly are you?" Mum asked, sounding relieved.

"At Jim Blackburn's place – he knows Mr Miller," I replied. "He said he'll put up the horses for the night."

"That's very handsome of him. But it still doesn't tell me where you are," Mum answered.

"Hang on. I'll find out," I said. I found Jim Blackburn talking to Angus. They'd removed the horses' saddles. The woman was making coffee in the kitchen. I asked Jim Blackburn to come and talk to Mum, only by that time it had become Dad.

"Are they furious?" Angus asked, when Jim

Blackburn had finished directing Dad and we were leading the horses to two loose boxes which were conveniently empty.

"No, I don't think so," I replied. "I think that Mum was just pleased to know that we were still in the land of the living."

We bedded down the boxes and fed and watered Frances and the bay mare. Then Jim Blackburn took us indoors and gave us each a mug of coffee with a dash of whisky, and the woman, who was fat and kind and called May, put a plate of scrambled eggs in front of us, and a loaf of fresh bread.

"Make yourselves at home. I'm slipping back out to the barn to see that your hunters are comfortable," Jim Blackburn said.

Angus leaped to his feet and cried, "Can't we help?" But we were firmly told to stay where we were and eat what we were given. The eggs had been scrambled in a frying pan and were delicious. May found us butter and preserves and we ate vast quantities of bread. I didn't enjoy my coffee much; I don't like it anyway, and the whisky made it taste even worse than usual.

"I hope Mum's rung up Wendy," Angus said. "It must have been terrible for her waiting by the truck."

The kitchen was warm and cosy. I felt incapable and sleepy. May seemed far away by the old-fashioned stove; the mugs hanging on the dresser were just a blur. Soon I slept, sprawled across the table.

I wakened to the sound of voices and a hand on my shoulder. "Jean, wake up. Come on, it's time to go home," Mum was saying. I had a crick in my neck and my legs felt stiff and heavy. For a moment I couldn't think where I was. Then it all came back.

"You've had a real good sleep," May said, with a smile which showed perfect teeth.

"It was that drop of whisky," Jim Blackburn said.

Mum seemed to be thanking everyone. I stood up and looked around the kitchen.

"You've been asleep for ages," Angus said. "We've just been looking at the horses; they seem quite happy."

I was still too sleepy to talk much. I remember shaking hands and saying thank you to May and Jim Blackburn in a kind of daze. Then I stumbled into the car and fell instantly asleep. In my dreams I heard the steady drone of Angus's voice explaining things to Mum.

Tea was still laid in the kitchen at Mountain Farm, but I was too tired to eat. I remember seeing that the clock on the window ledge said nine o'clock and I asked Mum if someone had told Wendy what had happened.

"Hours ago," she replied. "Dad's over there now."

I remember falling into bed, feeling the pillow against my face and with it a wonderful sense of security. I remember hearing Angus say, "Well, I'm going to have a bath anyway," and Mum saying "Shh." Then once again I slept, and this time it was the dreamless sleep of complete exhaustion.

10

On Sunday Joe drove Wendy, Angus and me over to Jim Blackburn's place in the truck. It was rather awkward meeting Wendy. Mr Miller had been extremely angry when she returned without us and as a punishment she wasn't to ride for a week. We had learned this from Dad. As a result Angus and I felt horribly guilty. In a way we knew that we were responsible for the punishment. Fortunately, Wendy isn't a person to harbour a grievance. She grinned when we met and called, "Sorry I let you down yesterday. I feel awful about it." After that we all blamed ourselves and set off in the truck in high spirits.

Wendy told us that she too had finished up miles from home on a tired horse. She had hacked back to the truck hoping to find us impatiently waiting; instead she had been met by a furious Joe, who said it was past six and he had his cow to milk when he got back. Wendy had insisted on waiting for half an hour, hoping that we might still turn up. She hadn't thought of ringing up home. Her father had telephoned Mountain Farm on her return. Later they had asked Mr Smythe to ring up if we appeared at his place. Wendy hadn't been able to eat until after I had telephoned Mum and everyone knew that we were at Jim Blackburn's place on the other side of the valley.

"I really think you had the worst time of all," Angus said, when Wendy came to the end of her story. "At least our adventures were exciting."

"Our families have got together and none of us are to hunt again until the boys are back. As if they ever look after anyone," Wendy told us.

"We must get our horses clipped," Angus replied. "That is, if we can still have them next holidays."

"That's just the heck of it. I just don't know what to say. You see, I'm too big to ride my little roan any more and Dad keeps saying we must have one of yours back," answered Wendy. She sounded apologetic and embarrassed. I said nothing. I hated the idea of losing either the bay mare or Frances, but we obviously couldn't keep both horses when Wendy had nothing to ride.

"Oh, well, perhaps we'll have caught the palomino by then. Anyway, don't worry, it won't be the first time we've managed with one mount between us, will it, Jean?" Angus said.

"Far from it," I agreed.

"I wish we could think of some way of stopping the beastly round-up," Angus said. "If only we could get off school."

"I don't see what we could do then," Wendy replied.

"Jeopardise the whole expedition somehow," Angus answered.

"Hey, some of them happen to be friends of mine," Wendy said.

"I didn't say I was going to hurt anybody," Angus replied.

I still felt sleepy. I think Wendy did too; there were dark rings under her eyes anyway and she kept passing her hand across her face, as though to ward off sleep.

It was another warm day. Jim Blackburn's place looked a haven of peace. A collie lay sunning himself in the stable yard; the horses were blinking and dreaming over their box doors. We found Jim Blackburn cleaning a bridle in a little room leading off the kitchen. He greeted us cheerfully and we all walked to the stables together. Frances and the bay mare looked tired. Their heads drooped and they were each resting one hind leg.

"They're sound all right. I led them both out first thing this morning. The bay mare's a wee bit stiff though," Jim Blackburn told us.

We led the horses into the truck from a

permanent loading ramp. Then I made the little speech Mum had suggested to me about paying for their board and lodging. But Jim Blackburn only laughed.

"Forget it," he said. "If I can't put up a couple of horses for a night without asking a fee, I'd better quit."

Joe was waiting. When he saw us he climbed into the cab of the truck and started the engine. We clambered into the back, just as it started with a jerk which sent us stumbling among the horses' legs. We all began to laugh when we were standing straight again. As we travelled home we discussed the wild horse. There seemed nothing we could do to stop the round-up.

"We'll just have to sit through school in agony, I suppose," Angus said, "imagining the palomino pitting his wits against a bunch of hard-hunting Virginian men."

"I'm jolly well going to suggest we have to-morrow off," I replied. "It's worth trying, anyway."

"We won't get it. Why should we?" Angus asked.

Finally, it was not until bedtime that I had the courage to ask that we might stay away from school the next day. The weekend guests had gone by then and a sudden peace had descended on Mountain Farm. We were sitting round a small fire in the dining-room. I asked with a sudden rush of words, and Mum said, "Why on earth should you?"

Dad said, "I do wish you would speak more slowly, Jean."

Angus explained about the round-up. "It's really tremendously important to us that we should forestall them," he finished.

"But what do you mean by forestall?" Dad asked.

"Find the wild horse before anyone else and drive him away from them," Angus answered promptly. I hadn't thought as far as that. I suppose it had been in Angus's head for some time.

"What a disgraceful idea. You really can't be so antisocial," Dad said.

"Don't you want us to catch the wild horse then?" I asked.

"I don't much mind either way. But I'm definite about one thing – you are going to school tomorrow," Dad replied.

I shall never forget Monday. On our way to school we met horsemen approaching the mountains by truck and horse box, trailer and car. We also saw a few lone riders crossing the valley, and dogs and a couple of hounds. There seemed little chance for the wild horse against so many. There was one consolation, no one as far as we could see carried a shotgun or rifle. There was a breeze blowing and the air felt light and free.

"What a wonderful morning for a round-up. I wish I was ten years younger," Mr Miller said.

"You're not so old. Let's have the radio on," Wendy suggested.

Mr Miller drove very fast, relying on his quick reactions and his brakes to save us should anything suddenly cross the road or dash out of a side turning.

My heart felt as heavy as lead. I was sure with the most complete certainty that the palomino would be captive before nightfall. I wondered whether the Millers would ask for the bay mare or Frances for the holidays. The remaining one would be very lonely living alone at Mountain Farm, I decided.

"Have you heard we're having a hunt breakfast on Christmas Day? The Jamesons are hunting. They've sent us an invitation," Wendy said.

"They always have an invitation meet on Christmas Day, and we thought it would be fun to give a hunt breakfast for everyone afterwards," Mr Miller explained.

"It will be a kind of farewell too. Because we're spending a week in New York after Christmas," Wendy said.

I felt Angus looking at me. It was the first time we had heard of anyone hunting on Christmas Day, or of the Millers visiting New York.

"Are they going to meet very early? I mean,

how does breakfast fit in?" Angus asked.

I felt disappointed. I had been looking forward to hunting with Pete and Phil. Now it seemed that they would be leaving for New York almost as soon as they arrived.

"After the hunt of course. They meet about ten," Wendy replied.

It sounded more like a hunt lunch or tea to me. I wondered what everyone ate for breakfast. I giggled and imagined all of us eating bowls of cereal.

"Everyone still comes in their hunting kit. It's very colourful," Mr Miller said.

I imagined muddy hunting boots trampling across the Millers' polished floors, the clink of spurs, the pink coats. "They send their horses home first of course," Mr Miller said.

I thought of tired horses climbing into vans and trucks jogging home, of grooms and second horsemen.

"They don't stay out long. Everyone's too darned keen to get back to their Christmas dinners," Mr Miller told us.

"It's just a kind of tradition. We have our traditions too, you see," Wendy said.

"It won't be a big affair. The last time we had a hunt breakfast there were ninety-five guests. Do you remember, Wendy?" Mr Miller asked.

"Sure," she replied.

"What are you going to New York for? Or is that being too nosey?" Angus asked.

"To visit the theatres, the movies and the galleries. We go every year," Wendy replied. By now we had reached our school.

"Be good," Mr Miller said, as we stepped out of the car and saw that we were late, and that the other children were all inside.

After school I was given a lecture by the headmaster. I had been reported three times for lack of attention. I tried to explain about the round-up and how important it was to me, but I don't think he understood. I didn't really listen to his lecture. I was longing to hear whether the wild horse was free or captive, nothing else seemed to matter. I heard that I was to stay in

during break for the next five days, and I was only pleased that I wasn't to stay after school. I rushed out to the car where the others were waiting. Mrs Miller had come to fetch us.

"What news?" I cried. "Have they caught him?"

"They hadn't by lunch-time. I haven't heard anything since," Mrs Miller replied.

"Isn't it awful? We still don't know," cried Angus in tones of exasperation.

"What did Mr Beeton say?" Wendy asked.

"Nothing much. Just that I'm to stay in during break for the next five days," I replied.

"Gee, tough luck," Wendy said.

There were no horse vans or trucks on the road. They must be still driving him, I thought, they must all be terribly tired.

"How can we find out? We must find out," Angus asked.

"Find out what?" Mrs Miller asked. "Oh, about that crazy horse. You're real obsessed about him, aren't you? It's not healthy, you know," she said.

We were nearly home now. I hoped that Mum would have news. Someone must know whether they had caught the wild horse or not. There was a feeling of rain in the air. The sky was grey. There was no one riding across the valley. There wasn't a dog in sight. The Hereford cattle grazed undisturbed.

Angus and I found Mum in the kitchen unpacking groceries.

"Is he caught?" cried Angus.

"Have you heard anything?" I asked.

Mum knew what we were talking about. "I haven't heard a sound since early morning. I inquired at the post office just now and they said they hadn't seen any horsemen since lunchtime," she replied.

Then the telephone rang. Angus answered. It was Wendy. I could hear her voice quite clearly from across the hall.

"We've just heard they haven't caught him. They're starting to go home now," she said.

I felt quite weak with relief. I leaned against the kitchen door and heard Wendy say, "They nearly caught him at eleven o'clock this morning down by the Hodges' farm, but after that they never had a chance. They got the mares all right, though."

"Well. Are you happy now?" asked Mum, who had heard the conversation from the kitchen. "You really mustn't let it become an obsession with you," she continued. "After all, he's not your horse." I wondered then whether Angus and I were really letting the wild horse become an obsession. It seemed odd that Mum and Mrs Miller should both say the same thing. Perhaps we are going nuts, I thought, and remembering how foolish I had been at school, I resolved to think less about the wild horse in future.

"Isn't it brilliant?" cried Angus, bursting into the kitchen. "He's defeated them all. He's still free."

"I know. We heard," I said. He does sound rather obsessed, I thought, looking at my brother.

The next three weeks passed slowly. Nothing happened. The wild horse seemed to have disappeared from the face of the earth. I received a long letter from Pete, full of questions about the cattle which I couldn't answer. The days grew shorter. The Millers started to feed hay and corn to the cattle. Mum began to mention Christmas.

We spent two evenings doing up parcels for England and writing in Christmas cards. At last everything for England was posted and we started to think of each other's presents and what we could give the Millers.

December came and with it the first frost. There was still no sign of the wild horse in the mountains. People didn't talk about it any more. It was as though the palomino had suddenly ceased to exist. Angus and I clipped the bay mare and Frances with the help of Joe and Wendy. Mr Miller lent us horse rugs. Mum, Angus and I made a Christmas pudding.

We received an invitation to the hunt breakfast, which we all accepted. The Millers were busy ordering food and polishing the house. Normally they hired extra staff and waiters for parties, but this time they couldn't because of it being Christmas.

At last, term ended. We drove home singing loudly. There were only five days left till Christmas. Late that evening Pete and Phil returned from the academy. They came down to see us at Mountain Farm. Phil seemed to have grown taller. He towered above us all. Pete seemed older and more serious. Dad gave them each a glass of beer and I found them some cake.

"So you haven't caught the wild horse," Pete said.

"I hear he's been bumped off," Phil told us.

"That's the first we've heard of it," Angus replied.

"He can't have been," I cried. I must have sounded desperate because suddenly everyone seemed to be looking at me.

"Don't take him seriously, Jean. He doesn't know a doggone thing," Pete told me.

"It's only what I heard at the drugstore when I stopped by for a Coke," Phil said.

At last we went to bed and, trying to sleep, I remembered the first time I had seen the wild horse, and my first glimpse of a Virginian moon, and the valley in the summer, warm and sunlit, and filled with the chorus of frogs in the lowlands.

We didn't see the Millers again till Christmas Day. Wendy had asked to have Frances back and we delivered her to Joe on Christmas Eve. "It's not going to be much fun having just one horse. We'll never catch the palomino now," Angus said.

I looked across the valley to the mountains faintly blue beneath the blue sky. "I wonder where he is. No one ever seems to see him now," I said. It seemed strange to talk about the wild horse again; afraid of being obsessed, we had hardly mentioned him for weeks.

"Perhaps Phil was right – perhaps he's been bumped off," Angus replied.

"Maybe he's moved to another valley," I said.

"Somehow I've stopped thinking he'll ever be ours. Everything seems so difficult," Angus said.

I wakened early on Christmas Day. My stocking was full and I seized it from the bottom of my bed before rushing into Angus's room. It was traditional that we should open our stockings together. There were all the usual things, even the tangerines in the toes of our stockings. The bay mare was neighing because she was on her own. We sat on Angus's bed and ate chocolate, nuts and tangerines. Outside it was snowing.

"I agree with Dad. I don't think Christmas Day and hunting go together," I said.

"You know that's only wishful thinking. If we'd been invited you would think quite differently," Angus replied with a grin. We got dressed, had breakfast of eggs and ham, and opened our presents.

I suddenly didn't want to go to the hunt breakfast. I never liked parties much and this was going to be a very grown-up sort of one. When we reached the Millers' the house was full of people. I avoided dancing and went with Pete to see his chestnut. He wanted to call it after me, but I managed to persuade him to call it Firefly. We stood and talked and talked, and in this way missed the rest of the hunt breakfast.

There were fourteen of us for dinner. There was wine in elegant glasses, turkey and sweet potato, asparagus, corn, bread sauce, and hot rolls in

front of each of us. The meal seemed to go on and on. I began to feel sleepy and Angus was gazing at me with a worried look on his face.

Some time much later Dad appeared and said, "Come on, we must go home. It's long past midnight."

"Well, did you enjoy yourselves?" Mum asked.

"It was okay. I liked the turkey," my brother answered.

"It went on too long," I said. It seemed ages since we had left home. It was very light in the valley. I looked across to the mountains now capped with snow. I thought of the wild horse roaming alone in a white world.

"Phil and Pete want me to go shooting with them tomorrow. They don't go to New York until the evening," Angus said.

"Oh lord," exclaimed Mum. "Do you think you're safe?"

"I've been shooting before," Angus replied.

"You must be sensible," Mum said anxiously.

The mountains looked cold and remorseless beneath the snow. I wondered what the wild horse would find to eat in his cold white world. He might be starving, I thought, gazing beyond the mountains to the cold grey sky.

"Everyone goes shooting, only they call it hunting, on Boxing Day. All the men, anyway," Angus said.

He may be hung up by his headcollar or trapped in a ravine, I decided, and suddenly I knew that, come what may, on the morrow I would search again for the wild horse.

"All right, you can go. But don't be foolish," Dad said to Angus. "Remember that a gun is a lethal weapon."

I dreamed all night about the wild horse: I was driving him down mountain passes blocked with snow and ice; I was schooling in the paddock at home in England; I was jumping him at Wembley . . .

I wakened to a white world and a cold pale sun. The sky was blue. The snow had stopped falling.

11

"You're shooting today," I told Angus the next day, Boxing Day, because he can't remember things early in the morning, and I knew he would be furious if he slept till ten o'clock by mistake.

Dad called, "Why are you up so early?" from the bedroom.

I couldn't stop to explain. I felt in a tremendous hurry. I wanted to be riding alone in the mountains, seeking the wild horse. "It's a quarter past eight," I answered, as I left the room and rushed downstairs. I mucked out the bay mare's box in ten minutes. Then I started to make toast for breakfast.

"What's the hurry?" Angus asked, yawning as he appeared in the kitchen. "It's not you who's shooting."

"I know. But I'm going to find the wild horse," I answered. "He may be starving."

"What, in this weather? Do you think you'll be allowed to go?" Angus asked. He sounded as though he didn't think it was very likely.

"I'm going, whatever anybody says. We can't leave him to starve. It's cruelty to animals," I replied.

"Be careful we don't shoot you. Anyway, I don't believe he's around here at all. Everybody thinks he's moved on," Angus said.

"Well, I'm just going to make sure," I replied. "And look what you've made me do," I shouted, as I spilt some milk.

"It's nothing to do with me. You've simply filled it too full," Angus said.

I felt all on edge, and I was terrified that my parents would forbid an expedition into the mountains.

"Why don't you come shooting? Wendy is," Angus said.

"No, thank you. I don't feel like killing things," I replied.

"Do you think Mum and Dad are ever going to get up? Shall we start without them?" I asked.

"Why don't you have breakfast and then get going before anyone comes down to say no? That's what I would do," Angus advised.

I knew that it was a bad suggestion but I couldn't bear the thought of not going. "Won't you get the blame then? I don't want you to be stopped shooting," I answered, making coffee.

"That doesn't matter. It's your expedition

which matters," my brother said. "Here, you go," he added, seizing a jug out of my hand. "I'll make the coffee."

I said "Thanks" and I snatched a hunk of bread, spread it with butter, and rushed out to the stable munching. I filled my pockets with oats and fetched a halter and the bay mare's tack.

Two minutes later I was mounting in the yard, "Good luck," Angus called softly from the back door.

I shouted "Thank you" and "Goodbye" but he had already returned to the kitchen. I hoped he wouldn't get into trouble.

I rode out of the yard into the white world. The snow was just crisp enough to avoid balling. The bay mare was fresh and wouldn't walk. I trotted briskly across the sparkling snow feeling as though I belonged to the distant past, before the advent of cars and the machine age.

The Hereford cattle were clustered around the Millers' farm waiting to be fed. Groundhogs and deer had left prints in the snow. The valley seemed empty and quite devoid of sound. It wasn't the valley I knew any more – just a vast white wilderness.

The trail leading into the mountains looked smaller and quite different beneath the snow. The snow coating the trees had thawed a little before it froze, so that now weird, fantastic icicles encased the branches like thick glass. The bay mare's hoofs made fresh prints in the snow, and it was obvious she and I were the first beings to tread the trail since Christmas night. There was the tiniest breeze which faintly stirred the encrusted leaves and made the trees creak uneasily; otherwise there was no sound and we might have been travelling through a dead world.

I thought of my parents eating breakfast at home; cracking the tops of boiled eggs, spreading toast with butter and marmalade. I hoped they weren't too angry at my behaviour, for though I was certain that I was on an errand of mercy, I was afraid they wouldn't see my expedition in the same light.

It was hard work following the trail; soon the bay mare was sweating and I was watching her ears to avoid the glare from the snow. I came to a fork and turned left for no particular reason. Here deer had left tracks in the virgin snow. My hands were cold in my bright new gloves and my feet were cold inside my boots. The sky had turned a miraculous blue, the sort of blue which belongs to the French Riviera, and the sun was melting the snow on the treetops. It was the sort of day and setting one dreams about.

I don't know how long I rode nor how far before I saw the first hoofprints in the snow, and knew that my hunch was right and that somewhere not far away the wild horse walked alone through the mountains. I began to feel excited because I knew that my journey was justified and that there was hope again on the horizon. I hurried the bay mare and I think she knew that we were near our goal, for she seemed to take new heart.

Soon I heard the distant sound of firing and, in my imagination, I saw the Millers and Angus ploughing through the snow with guns. Then the hoofprints left the trail and we were plodding through undergrowth and under trees and over half-buried rocks. I think the bay mare could smell the palomino, for she seemed to follow the hoofprints with great eagerness and once or twice she stopped to smell the air.

I started to wonder what would happen when the wild horse saw us. I dreaded an exciting chase. Where the snow was melting in the sunshine it formed into hard balls in the bay mare's hoofs and several times she stumbled and almost fell. Once she seemed to be walking on stilts, and I was about to dismount when the ball fell out and lay a dirty grey lump on the white snow.

I had been lost for some time when we reached a tiny clearing and saw, standing alone beneath a tree, a horse coated with snow and ice. It was the palomino, but he looked quite different. He seemed half asleep and icicles hung from his mane and fetlocks, his ribs showed through the snow on his sides, and his eyes were partly closed and dull as though life didn't interest him any more. In spite of his awful appearance, my heart gave a leap of joy, for at last I had found him, at least he was still alive.

He raised his head a little as we approached, and the bay mare whinnied softly. A tattered headcollar hung on his tired head. I'd never seen a horse look so weary before. I was nearly crying as I dismounted from the bay mare. I felt no triumph at all.

I said, "Hello, whoa little horse," as I approached the palomino, and though his tired eyes watched me warily, he didn't move. I knew then that he was very sick. I reached out a hand and took a piece of rope which dangled from his headcollar and still he didn't move. I saw that his eyes were almost yellow and so were his nostrils and his mouth. I wondered whether he was strong enough to make the journey home. I tied the halter I had brought on to his headcollar and brushed the snow off his thin, drooping neck. The bay mare rubbed her head against him, but he gave no response.

He wouldn't eat the oats out of my pockets. I rubbed his cold, half-frozen ears and I could feel him falling to sleep again. Somehow I had to get him home, he would never stand another

night in the mountains. I guessed that he had come to the clearing in the small hours and that he hadn't moved since; it looked as though it had been his home for some time.

I stood and wished that I had Angus with me

and that I was in England and could reach a telephone in a few minutes and get hold of a horse box. I wished that Pete was with me because I was sure he would know how to handle the situation. I felt very helpless alone in the mountains with the two horses. My hands were numb and snow from the few thawing trees had dripped down my neck. At that moment I hated Virginia and the Blue Ridge Mountains more than anywhere else in the world. I hated the icicles and the snow and the endless trails which all looked just alike. I hated the sky, the sun and the remoteness, and the few birds hovering in the air looking for dying animals to eat.

Wendy had told me once about these birds. She called them an omen of death. Now they were just above, cawing greedily – a hungry flock of birds waiting for the palomino to die.

When I saw the birds I knew I couldn't leave the palomino and seek help. I was frightened that they would swoop while I was away and when I returned I would find only a heap of newly picked bones. I had heard that these birds didn't wait for animals to die, only until they were too weak to fight any more, then they descended and the mountains echoed with the screams of the dying animal.

The birds made up my mind for me. I pulled gently on the halter and said, "Come on, phantom horse, we're going home." The covering of snow made him look like a phantom – a phantom on his last pilgrimage.

The bay mare encouraged him with another whinny. I think she knew how ill he was. At last my words and the pull on his headcollar seemed to reach his brain, he moved with awkward, stiff steps, as though his limbs were frozen. He was so pitiful that I cried and my tears made little holes in the snow. I had to go back the way I had come because it was the only way I knew.

I followed the bay mare's hoofprints back through the undergrowth, under the trees and over the rocks. Every few minutes I had to stop to let the palomino rest. It was ages before I reached the trail again.

Then I saw that the weather had changed. The sun had gone. The sky was no longer blue, but the sort of grey which means snow. The air was much warmer and I knew that I had to hurry because soon there would be fresh snow which would obliterate the hoofprints and then I would be really lost. Already the snow was soft on the trail. I sank in deeply each time I took a step and my jodhpurs and boots were soon soaking wet. I walked between the two horses, the bay mare hurried and the palomino lagged and it wasn't a pleasant journey.

And then the snow came in large, white flakes. It fell on my hair, on the horses, on the trail and the trees and undergrowth, it fell as though it would never stop falling.

I thought of the time, of my parents waiting anxiously at home. I began to wonder whether I should ever reach the warmth and safety of Mountain Farm. Nobody was shooting any more. The mountains were wrapped in silence except for the eerie sound of falling snow, all prints had vanished, nothing seemed to live except myself and the two horses.

I started to wish that I had brought provisions. My tummy told me that it was lunch-time; my legs felt weak and I longed for a bar of chocolate or a large ham sandwich. I tried to heighten my morale by imagining the palomino in the stable at home, but when I looked at him and saw his utter weariness I started to wonder whether he would live if we ever did reach home.

I shall never forget the next few hours. We plodded on and on and the trail looked just the same. The bay mare started to tire and to look back as though we had taken the wrong turning and were now walking directly away from home. I began to worry. I saw night falling, and snow deepening. I wondered whether my parents would send out a search-party. I felt terribly guilty, and for a moment I wished I hadn't listened to Angus's advice in the morning; then I looked at the palomino again and suddenly I didn't regret anything any more. It was so wonderful to think that if he lived he would really be ours.

I thought of hunting him across a russet and gold Virginian countryside, of seeing him from my window early in the morning and knowing that he was ours, of feeding him late at night and riding him in the spring. I saw us jumping in shows, competing in hunter trials, bringing home the tri-coloured rosette. I saw myself rounding up cattle on him with Phil and Pete, schooling him in the paddock at home, I saw him wearing elegant rugs with our initials in one corner. I plodded on through the snow lost in my own happy imagination, ceasing to notice my aching legs, the feeling of afternoon, or the endlessly falling snow.

Dusk came quite suddenly. It came with a darkening sky and a whispering evening breeze. I had followed the same trail for hours, yet nothing seemed changed. Both horses were dragging by this time, and I'm sure they knew I was lost. When I halted, the palomino stood drearily with hanging head, and a sickly eye which showed no interest at all in anything. I looked down the trail and, reasoning that we must reach somewhere some time, I plodded on. The wind blew the snow in our faces and my eyes started to run, and my gloves were wet from where the snow had melted when it met the warmth of my hands. I started to sing to raise my spirits. I sang pop-songs and songs from musicals. Then I began singing hymns.

Because of the snow, night came without darkness. And then, quite suddenly, I saw twinkling lights shining through the trees. I started to hurry and shouted to the horses, "Come on. We're getting somewhere at last." But they wouldn't hurry; they had lost all confidence in me. They dragged and the snow balled more and more in their hoofs, and they stumbled and jerked my arms, while I pulled frantically on the rope and the reins, losing all sense and reason in a wild desire to reach the twinkling lights.

Then I thought of shouting. "I'm coming. Is there anyone about? I've caught the wild horse," I called, and my voice echoed and came back muffled by the falling snow.

I hurried on and gradually the lights seemed nearer. The snow was very deep now, soft and wet, so that it was hard work moving at all.

Then I thought I heard an answering call, and I started to shout twice as loudly. "It's Jean, I'm all right, I've got the wild horse," I yelled over and over again.

Soon I could feel a stronger breeze blowing through the trees and, quite suddenly, there was more light and space. We had reached a valley and, with a cry of joy, I saw that it was our valley.

I tried to run and fell sprawling in the snow. The horses waited patiently until I was on my feet again; the bay mare raised her head and looked across the valley to where the lights shone bravely in Mountain Farm.

I remember hoping that there would be someone at home when I arrived. I was terrified lest the whole district should be out searching for me. And now I saw that there were lots of little lights moving about the valley. There were tiresome little gusts of snow, and drifts. I started to shout, "I'm coming, I'm coming, I'm coming," until the words were all jumbled together and didn't make sense any more.

The bay mare was hurrying now. She jogged and bumped the palomino and he stumbled and almost fell. I slackened my pace, I didn't want to take a dead horse home.

I talked to the palomino. "Soon you'll be in a lovely warm stable, a really super one," I told him. "There'll be lots to eat and gradually you'll get well again."

I stopped and patted him and rubbed his ears and he stood with his legs sprawled apart as though he couldn't move another step. If it had been possible to get a horse box to him I think I would have left him there, but as it was I had to keep him moving.

Then I thought I heard a shout and I started to call again. Someone called, "It's Jean. She's

reached the valley." After that there was a great
deal of shouting and suddenly a bell rang out
loud and clear, drowning the voices. Lights
seemed to be moving towards me from all direc-
tions and the bay mare was dragging me faster
and faster towards Mountain Farm, and, somewhere behind me, the palomino was dragging
on my other arm until I thought it must fall
from its socket. I kept yelling, "It's Jean. I'm
home," till someone said quite close, "It's all
right now, we know," and I saw my brother
and beyond him the back door standing open.

"I've got the wild horse," I said. "But he's terribly ill. I think we should have the vet at once. He's almost dead. That's why I've been so long." I started to cry, because the palomino really did look ill, and I was suddenly sure that he wouldn't last more than a few hours because his eyes looked sunken in their sockets and he was hardly breathing any more.

"Let's get him inside," Angus said.

"Where are Mum and Dad?" I asked.

"Looking for you," Angus replied, taking the bay mare. "It's all right. They will have heard the bell, that was to be the signal."

"You mean that I was home?" I asked, and Angus nodded.

The palomino tottered into the empty loose box. He seemed to be in a coma. I don't think he had any idea where he was.

I shut the box door. "I'll ring up a vet," I said. I felt I must do it immediately, before my parents arrived and I had to explain.

I asked the operator to put me through to the nearest vet, and the girl who answered said, "Will Dr Beecher do?"

I almost replied, No, I want a vet, not a doctor, before I remembered that vets are called doctors in America. "Sure. Fine," I answered.

I saw that the snow on my clothes was melting in pools on the hall floor. Then Dr Beecher answered and I told him what had happened, speaking as slowly and coherently as I could. When I had finished speaking, he said, "Okay, I'll be right over," and hung up. I thought of him hurrying for his coat, starting his car. Then I began to wonder whether he would ever reach us on such a night.

Angus had settled the bay mare when I returned to the stable. She had piles of straw under her rugs and was munching a hot feed.

"I had it all ready," he said. "But I don't know what to do about the palomino. He won't eat a thing."

"He's awfully ill. Have you noticed how yellow he is?" I asked.

"Let's hope the vet can do something," my brother replied.

"Hello, are you there, Jean?" someone called, and I saw my parents wading through the snow.

"Yes, I'm back. I've got the wild horse. He's terribly ill. I think he's dying. That's why I've been so long."

I was afraid they would be angry. But Dad said, "We thought it was something like that."

And Mum said, "If only you would choose better weather for your expeditions. But perhaps now you've got the wretched horse, you'll stop giving us frights."

"I'm terribly sorry. I didn't mean to stay out so long," I replied.

"It doesn't matter," Mum answered.

There were more voices now and Pete, Phil and Wendy came into the yard.

"Congratulations, Jean," Pete said, taking my hand.

"He's terribly ill," I replied quickly. "He may die. I've rung up the vet. He's coming right over." I didn't want congratulations. I didn't think bringing a sick horse home was a deed which deserved congratulations – it's something you do expecting no reward, I thought. Besides, no one with a heart could have left the palomino to die in the mountains.

"You'd better come in and change. You look soaked," Mum said.

"What about the palomino? He shouldn't be left alone," I cried.

"We'll look after him," Dad answered. "Hurry up and have a hot bath and get some food inside you. Then we can talk."

I went indoors with Mum and she pulled off my wet jodhpurs and I suddenly discovered that I was terribly tired and ravenously hungry.

I ate some bread and butter and had a hot bath and changed. There was hot soup waiting for me in the kitchen and braised ham and potatoes.

Angus was leaning against the stove. "The vet hasn't come yet. I've sent the Millers home," he told me. "Wendy would talk and the palomino needs quiet."

"I thought they were going to New York," I replied.

"The weather's stopped them. The road's blocked near Baltimore," Angus said.

"Did you have a good shoot?" I asked, remembering the morning, which seemed so long ago.

"No, the snow was too deep. By the way, I told Mum and Dad that you probably wouldn't be back to lunch. That's why they didn't start worrying till teatime."

I looked at the clock and saw that it was six o'clock. I had imagined that it was nearly suppertime. "Were they furious?" I asked.

"They were rather," Angus answered. "They said that you were going potty over the wild horse."

Mum and Dad came in from the stables.

"He does look in a bad way. I think I'll ring up Smythe. He'd better know we've got his horse," Dad told us.

"Jean's horse now," Angus replied.

"Yours, too. Because if it hadn't been for you I wouldn't have gone," I told Angus.

It was ages before Dr Beecher came. We had all eaten supper by that time, taking it in turns to watch the palomino. Dad had talked to Mr Smythe for hours on the telephone, and we knew now that if the palomino lived he would be ours for ever and ever.

At last there was a knock on the back door and a small man clutching a black bag stood in the yard.

"I'm real sorry I've been so long. I've walked the last three miles, the road's completely blocked by the snow," he said.

I liked Dr Beecher at once. We all hurried to the stable where Angus was watching the palomino. The vet didn't talk much.

He murmured, "Gee, he's bad. He's eaten something really bad." Then he mentioned poison and jaundice, and found the palomino had a temperature of a hundred and five. He gave

him three injections and stood and looked at him for some time.

"There's nothing more we can do tonight but hope," he said at last. "I'll stop by first thing tomorrow."

"Are you sure you wouldn't like to stay the night?" Mum asked.

"Thank you, ma'am. I guess I'd better not. Maybe I'll get some more calls tonight," Dr Beecher replied. We were very quiet when he had left.

"Well, that's that. We can do no more," Dad said.

"What were the injections?" Angus asked.

"Penicillin, iron and liver – or some sort of food or vitamins – I don't know what the other one was," Dad replied.

"He's bringing some sort of drench in the morning," Mum said.

We looked at the palomino before we went to bed. He was lying down and he looked happier, though still terribly ill.

"Do you think he will live?" I asked Dad.

"Who can tell? We can only hope, as Dr Beecher said," Dad replied.

I hated going to bed. Outside the snow was still falling. It seemed sad to have caught the wild horse at last and not to know whether he would live or die. Not that I cared very much whose horse he was – I only wanted him to live. I prayed for him before I fell asleep.

I remember Angus coming into my room and saying, "If he lives, let's call him Phantom, because he looked like a phantom coming across the valley with you tonight all covered with snow and thin and out of another world."

"All right," I answered. "If he lives."

And now everything is nearly told. For the palomino lived; after three days of hovering between life and death, he stood on his legs again and looked over his loose box door.

As Angus suggested, we named him Phantom, and, perhaps because of our English accents or perhaps because we rescued him, he seems to love Mountain Farm and whinnies when he sees us, and is much loved by us all.

Since Phantom came to live with us, Angus and I have become much nicer and far more sensible. We don't get lost any more because he always knows the way home; and we don't lose our heads, because now he's ours there doesn't seem to be anything worth pursuing through the ever-changing Blue Ridge Mountains of Virginia.

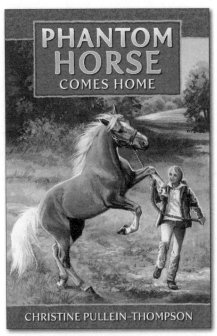

ISBN 978-1-84135-822-2

PHANTOM HORSE
COMES HOME

*"I'm not going to leave without Phantom!
I refuse to leave!"*

When Jean learns that her family is soon
to move back to England, all she can think
about is Phantom, the wild palomino
horse she has tamed. Will she have
to leave him behind?

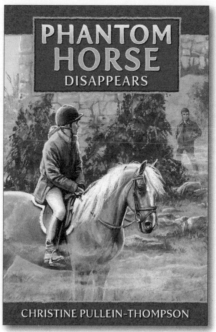

ISBN 978-1-84135-821-5

PHANTOM HORSE
DISAPPEARS

*"You're fools! Why couldn't
you leave things are they were?
Why did you come here?"*

When Jean and Angus discover the
terrible secret of Aunt Mary's house,
they are caught up in a dangerous plot
to kidnap their beloved Phantom.

ISBN 978-1-84135-824-6

PHANTOM HORSE
IN DANGER

I imagined Phantom twisting, kicking, rearing, ropes round his quarters, a blindfold over his eyes. The thought sent tears running down my cheeks like rain.

When their horses are in mortal danger, Jean and Angus hatch a desperate plan to save them. Will they be in time?

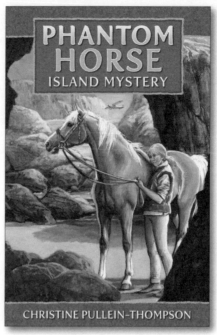

ISBN 978-1-84135-825-3

PHANTOM HORSE
ISLAND MYSTERY

The idyllic island where Jean takes
Phantom with her on holiday hides a
dangerous mystery. Why have most of
the inhabitants left, and why are horses
being secretly flown to the island?

When Jean is plunged into another
perilous adventure, can Phantom save her?

ISBN 978-1-84135-823-9

PHANTOM HORSE
WAIT FOR ME

*"Jean, darling, there's no point locking
yourself in your room. It won't bring
Phantom back…"*

When Phantom goes missing, little does
Jean suspect that her horse is the bait
in a plot to capture her. In a race for
their lives, will they escape in time?

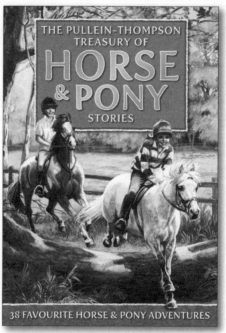

ISBN 978-1-84135-804-8

THE PULLEIN-THOMPSON
TREASURY OF
HORSE & PONY
STORIES

Packed with exciting adventures, this
bumper collection from the world's best-loved
horse storytellers will delight horse and pony
lovers everywhere.